IRISHED

THE INVINCIBLES

BOOK SEVEN

USA TODAY BESTSELLING AUTHOR

HEATHER SLADE

IRISHED
© 2021 Heather Slade

ISBN: 978-1-953626-14-1

irished

/ahy-risht/

verb

to start off great, and then fizzle out

MORE FROM AUTHOR HEATHER SLADE

Table of Contents

Prologue

Irish
Crested Butte, Colorado
June

Buck led the other people we were traveling with and me into the ranch's main house.

"Hello?" he called out.

"Hey, Buck," I heard a female's voice answer; she walked up and hugged him.

"Where is everybody?" he asked.

"Out surveying." The woman turned and looked directly at me. "Who are you?"

"Paxon Warrick," I said, stepping forward and extending my hand. When she took it, a feeling I couldn't explain, other than to say I never wanted to let go, washed over me.

"Flynn Wheaton," she said. Her cheeks flushed, and I gripped her hand tighter.

"Great name."

"Yours too."

When Buck touched her arm, I dropped Flynn's hand and watched as she met and shook the hands of the other people in the room. More than once, I saw her look over her shoulder at me.

I knew from the brief I'd received that Buck only had one sister, which meant Flynn was twenty-one years old. What I'd give to take ten years off my age and be five years older than her rather than fifteen.

When most everyone other than me, Buck, and one person besides Flynn left, she walked over to me. When she looked into my eyes with her mesmerizing blue ones, all thoughts of age faded into irrelevance.

I longed to reach out and run my fingers through her long hair that was light brown with golden highlights. When she turned her head just slightly, I saw shades of red too.

Flynn took a deep breath when I stepped closer. I opened my mouth to speak, but words escaped me. If she and I were alone, I'd tell her how beautiful she was. But we weren't, as I was immediately reminded when her brother, who'd left momentarily, returned.

"Ready?" he said to me.

"I should head out now too, but I'm sure I'll see you later," said Flynn, seemingly jarred out of the same trance I was in.

"I'd like that." I followed her to the front door and watched her walk away, wishing, maybe for the first time ever, that I could leave the wretched hell my life had become and follow.

Part I

1

I'd been at The Farm—official name Camp Peary—for a little over two months when another recruit, Sumner Copeland, arrived. He was the son of a senator and, in general, a pain in my fucking ass.

Even though I was eight weeks ahead of him, there wasn't a single training exercise, physical or mental, where he didn't best me. What made it worse was that our instructors appeared to be pitting us against one another, something I hadn't seen them do with any other recruits.

After two weeks of that bullshit, both Copeland and I were called into the big boss' office. I was stunned by what he told us.

"Irish," he began, using the nickname I'd received my first day there, when the in-processing agent told me Paxon was a "pussy" name, "Cope here will be acting as your handler from here on out."

I looked at Cope and then at the boss, knowing I had two choices. I could accept his decision or leave. What I couldn't do was argue.

I'd been counting the days—one hundred and twenty-four, to be exact—until I could finish my training and never see Cope's smug face again. So, what did the boss' announcement mean? "Define here on out."

The boss cocked his head. "For as long as you both work for the CIA, son."

"No fucking way!" I screamed inside my head, smart enough not to say it out loud. "Does this mean he's my superior?" I felt like a jackass as soon as I asked. I mean, I should know what a "handler" does, right?

The boss rested his arms on the desk and leaned forward. "It means he's responsible for making sure you have every single thing you need to accomplish your mission and live to accept the next."

Which meant, if he fucked up, I was the one who died.

"Any other questions?"

"No, sir," Cope answered before I could.

I repeated his words, and we both stood to leave.

"Listen," Cope began when we were outside the building. "I want you to know this wasn't my idea."

"I didn't think it was."

"I'm too much of a risk to put out in the field. If I weren't assigned as a handler, I would've been tossed out of the program."

I highly doubted that was the case. "Why?"

"My father. Major handicap, my whole fucking life."

The last words, he muttered, but I heard him, and for whatever reason, it made me like him more.

"This is all about trust, Irish."

"Right." On my part anyway. What did he have to lose? Sounded to me like he'd be sitting behind a desk while I risked my life.

Cope looked as though there was something else he wanted to say, but I didn't encourage him to continue. Only time would tell whether I would feel the trust that this was all about.

2

Flynn
Crested Butte, Colorado
Thirteen Years Ago

As much as I never, ever wanted my oldest brother to leave, I knew he had to. All he and our dad did was fight. Porter, who was the next oldest after Buck, said they always had, especially after our mom died.

I was only three at the time and didn't remember anything about her. There were pictures of her around the ranch house, and my brothers told stories, but I had no memories of my own.

"Hey, squirt," said Cord, brother number three in oldest to youngest in our family. "You hangin' in there okay?"

I looked up from the book I was reading.

"You need anything, you let me know. Understand?"

"I understand." I wouldn't go to him, though, if I needed anything. I'd either ask my brother Holt, since he was closer to my own age, or Johnny, the head cook at the dining hall where my father usually had me hang out when he and my brothers were busy on the ranch.

Since I started kindergarten, Holt and I had gone to the same school and he always looked out for me. Next year, he would go to middle school and I'd be left on my own. Just thinking about it, made my stomach hurt. Now, I was only made fun of when the other kids knew my brother wasn't around. Once he was in a different building, it would be all the time.

"Hey, heifer!" they'd shout and then moo at me when there was no teacher within hearing distance. I hated it, but less because it hurt my feelings. It was the humiliation that made my cheeks heat and my stomach ache.

I'd begged Holt not to say anything about it to our older brothers or our dad, and he never had. Maybe he was afraid, like I was, that our father would think it was funny. Worse, he might start calling me that himself. Every so often, I could swear I heard him making pig sounds when he caught me in the kitchen, getting a snack.

My dad was all about perfection. At least the outward appearance of it. I was anything but perfect. I hated the jeans and western shirts he bought for me. I might as well be his fifth son, the way I looked in them. And my hair? I kept it tied back in a ponytail all day and night. When he thought it was too long, he'd just cut part of it off.

"Whatcha doin'?" I heard my brother Buck ask.

"Nothing," I said, barely turning my face from the pillow I'd been crying into.

"You know if there was any way I could take you to college with me, I would, Flynn."

I dried my tears on the pillowcase and looked up at him, relieved he thought I was crying over him rather than feeling sorry for myself.

3

Irish
Hong Kong
Nine Years Ago

The mission we were assigned was standard reconnaissance. As the person with the least seniority, I was given the worst shifts and shittiest jobs. I didn't mind. I knew one day there would be someone else below me. Fair was fair.

My three partners for tonight's duty were Peter "Dingo" Samuels, Albert "337" Baker, and Eric "Julius" Berg. The three had a lot more seniority than me, but since they were looking to leave the mission early, they'd volunteered for the "swing" shift.

The man we were watching, a Chinese-born Canadian national, was the suspected kingpin of a vast drug network that was raking in upwards of fifty million dollars annually.

He wasn't on our watch list because the CIA wanted to bring him in. Our mission was to determine who his main points of contact were in Hong Kong and who was laundering his money.

As danger went, it was relatively low risk, given we had no authority whatsoever to act, only to report information.

The streets were empty but for a few vagrants as we waited for our relief team. Two men, though, caught my eye as they rounded a corner and stood there, looking in our direction long enough that it raised my concern.

"Dingo—" I'd no more said his name than a vehicle sped past, taking out all three of the agents I was on duty with. Samuels fell face-first into the alley from which we'd been conducting our stakeout. The other two were farther away, but there was no question they were dead. All that prevented me from meeting the same fate was that I'd been standing in the shadows, hidden by the corner of the building.

"Agents down," I hissed into my mic. "Repeat. Agents down."

What happened over the course of the next three days left my head spinning. No one asked me for an account of what I saw or heard. The entire mission was scrubbed, then burned.

And Dingo, 337, and Julius? I never heard their names mentioned again.

My mother used to say every person dies three deaths. The first is when the body ceases to function. The second is when that body is put in the grave. The third is when your name is spoken for the last time. Seemed to me that all three happened on the same day for the three men I'd been working with.

When I returned Stateside, I asked Cope to meet me away from the office.

"It came way too close, man," I told him. "It was a low-risk mission."

"What I don't understand is why it was burned at all, let alone so fast."

"I agree."

Cope said he'd dig around and see if he could find any other information, but I could tell he was as skeptical about his success as I was.

4

Exactly when I'd started keeping track of agents', operatives', and assets' deaths, I couldn't remember. As I added names to my ongoing tally, I added more details. Soon, I began adding photos along with as much information as I could about how and where they had been assassinated.

That's what I called it. These men and women didn't "die in the line of duty," as was sometimes reported, and then only within the company. The general public never knew a thing about those who had given their all to protect our collective freedom. I did, though.

The spare bedroom of my condo became a cross between a shrine and a war room. The walls were covered with notes, and whenever I filled a whiteboard, I added at least two more.

I divided the room's four walls into where the agents were originally from. Most were either from the States, the UK, and either France or Germany, which I lumped together. The fourth wall became "everyone else." It wasn't necessary for me to sort them by where they'd died. With few exceptions, it was either in Hong Kong or mainland China.

Was I obsessed? Sure. Especially after another instance—in Beijing—where agents I was working with were gunned down and the entire mission burned.

Each person whose likeness hung on my walls could've been me. Particularly given I'd come so close on not one but two occasions.

It was what had made me start paying attention. The deaths I'd witnessed had nothing to do with our mission, as far as I could tell. It seemed almost random, but everything else about it, including the agency's reaction, didn't.

There had to be a connection, and before I faced the same fate as so many others, I had to find out what it was.

Tonight wouldn't be the first time Cope stopped by my place for a beer. We didn't make a habit of it; there were weeks we couldn't stand the sight of each other. I didn't have any siblings, and neither did he, so I couldn't say I felt the same way about him as I would a brother. But maybe.

He held up a six-pack when I opened the door and waved him in.

"Thanks for stopping by."

Cope pulled one bottle out of the carrier and was about to open it, but set it on the table. "What's going on?"

I walked over, opened the beer, and handed it to him. "Have a drink."

He took a swig. "This isn't going to be a 'shoot the shit and avoid talking about anything to do with the job' night, is it?"

I chugged the beer I'd poured into a glass and shook my head. "There's something I need to show you."

"I don't like the sound of this."

"You're going to like it even less when you see it."

He sighed in that asshole-y, condescending way he did that pissed me the fuck off. "Irish—"

"Shut up, Cope. Whatever you're about to say, I guarantee you'll regret it. In fact, I'd advise you to just keep your mouth zipped until I explain."

As Cope had said that fateful day when he was assigned to me—or vice versa—the thing about a handler and one of his agents is that it's all about trust. As much as Cope could make me crazy, at the end of every single day, I trusted him and he trusted me.

I opened another beer for myself, and he did the same. "Come with me." I turned the handle on the door that always remained closed and took a deep breath.

"Irish? What the fuck—"

"Sit down."

He sat, opened his mouth, closed it, and opened it again. I sat too and kept quiet as I watched him scan the room. His expression changed as he realized what was written beneath the images were dates of death.

"Paxon—"

I held up my hand. I wasn't ready to speak and didn't want him to, either. Whenever I entered this room, I forced myself to take several moments of still and reverent silence.

When I was a kid, I went to a Holocaust museum on a school field trip. Our entire class, usually boisterous, was solemn as we studied the images and realized what they represented. This was the same. Each image was a life lost. Worse, it was a name forgotten by those who should've honored their memory.

Before standing, I took a deep breath. I walked over to the first wall.

Cope stood too and walked closer. He pointed to the three images above the names. "These are the guys who died on your mission," he said.

"That's right. Peter Samuels, Albert Baker, and Eric Berg. All died in the line of duty two years ago in Hong Kong."

Cope slowly walked around the room, scanning images, reading the notes I'd written about each one. When he got to the fourth wall, he turned to me. "How many?"

"Number fifty died last week."

"Jesus. Fifty," he repeated under his breath. "Why haven't you shown me this before?"

I had no answer. I didn't know why I chose to now. Until he arrived, I had no intention of doing so. Maybe it was the tally reaching a milestone number that made it too hard to bear on my own anymore. Maybe I wanted someone besides me to know. To remember. And maybe, if I met the same fate they had, I wanted Cope to find out why. Why had more agents died in the last three years than in the twenty prior combined?

5

Irish
Washington, DC
Six Years Ago

It had been three years since Cope and I began the mission we undertook with no authority or funding, both of us knowing our careers as well as our lives were on the line if anyone found out about it.

Thus far, every theory we contrived led nowhere. If it weren't for the sheer number of deaths that couldn't be explained or attributed to anything, it would be easy to think it a tragic coincidence. Except I couldn't do that. Agents I'd worked with directly had been gunned down in front of me. I was convinced their deaths had nothing to do with the op we were on, and yet nothing about them was random.

The only apparent link was that three sets of murders I'd witnessed took place either in Beijing or Hong Kong. Two were close calls for me too. One, I was at a safe distance away, but the end result was still the same—agents were dead and no one had any idea why.

Without any other leads, the Chinese became the center of our investigation. Given relations between our two countries were strained even more than with Russia, it wouldn't be a stretch of anyone's imagination to believe either communist nation was behind the loss of so many of our agents.

While, to a certain extent, Cope influenced the missions I was assigned, he certainly wasn't the person who ultimately decided what they were. That was a couple of steps above his pay grade. He did make sure, though, that I was put front and center for every mission related to China—including those in Hong Kong.

Most of my other assignments had enough downtime that I could continue looking for patterns in what appeared to be systemic execution. There had to be something that tied the deaths together—other than China, which both Cope and I believed worthy of more investigation. How they were involved specifically, though, remained a perplexing mystery.

Today, like every other time we met on the subject, we were careful about where and when we talked. We set off from the CIA headquarters in separate cars and drove an hour to Annapolis, Maryland. Once there, we left our cell phones in our vehicles, met at the public docks, and rented a boat.

It was a warm mid-September day that felt more like summer than the beginning of autumn, so we chartered a thirty-two-foot cruiser. Once we were far enough out in the Chesapeake Bay, Cope cut the engine.

"Does the name Malin Kilbourne mean anything to you?"

"She's one of the agents you handle, right? Code name Starling."

"That's right." Cope looked over his shoulder. There was nothing but water within a couple hundred yards of us. "She's picked up a lead on something I'm going to let her run with."

"Let her run with? Isn't she brand spanking new?"

"To me, yeah, but she trained under Dutch Miller. She's got chops." Cope looked over both shoulders a second time. "I'll monitor her closer than she realizes."

"What the fuck has she gotten herself mixed up in that has you so tightly wound that you keep looking over your shoulder?"

"Somebody from DHS gave her a tip on money coming into a super PAC."

I knew there had to be a hell of a lot more to it than that. "Get to the point, Cope."

"She starts looking into it, and within a couple of days, Ed Montgomery steps in and assigns her a mission in Afghanistan."

"Whoa. Back up. Isn't he with Congressional Affairs?"

"Yep."

I cocked my head, trying to figure out why someone Cope didn't report to was giving missions to an agent he handled.

"Is there a new chain of command I'm unaware of?"

Cope shook his head. "Right? Striker asked me what the fuck I thought I was doing."

"And?"

"I told him to ask Stevens." Striker Ellis was Cope's and my boss. Ellis reported to Paul Stevens, who was the head of the National Clandestine Service branch of the CIA. Stevens answered directly to James Flatley, Director of the CIA. Ed Montgomery was nowhere in that chain of command.

"What did Stevens say?" I asked.

"He told Striker to stay in his lane."

"Striker? Not Montgomery?"

"You heard right."

"Whatever this super PAC is, someone doesn't want Starling poking her nose into it."

"Don't call her that, by the way. She hates it," said Cope.

"So, what's the deal with the super PAC?"

"No clue. All information about it has been burned."

"What's Kilbourne know?"

"I'm going to let her lead me to it."

"You don't think she's going to drop this even though she's been assigned something else."

"Hell, no."

"What's her mission, anyway?"

"Infiltrate the Islamic State."

I shook my head and looked out over the water, finally understanding why Cope and I were discussing Starling and the super PAC. "Montgomery wants her out of the picture—permanently."

"You got it."

"How closely are you monitoring her?"

"Close enough that if someone kills her, I'll have a lead on who's behind it."

"But not close enough to stop it."

"Look, Irish, she's one of how many now?"

I didn't respond. In three years, the list had grown from fifty to sixty-four. Sacrificing one more, even if it led us to why agents were being killed and by whom, wasn't something I could condone. I didn't give a shit about the greater good.

"Irish?"

"Fuck off, Cope."

"Come on, you have to agree it's what needs to be done."

I turned my head and leveled my gaze at him. "I will never agree. Never."

6

Flynn
Crested Butte, Colorado
Four Years Ago

In the eight years since my brother Holt and I went to the same school at the same time, the bullying and taunting had gotten progressively worse to the point where I considered either dropping out of school or running away. Some weeks it got so bad, I thought about killing myself.

The worst part was that the more they called me a fat cow, the more I ate, and the more weight I put on.

Recently, along with the heifer jokes, my classmates had also started calling me a lesbian. While most of the girls in my class had outgrown their own tomboy stages, I hadn't. For me, it wasn't as much about outgrowing it as having no means to look more like a girl.

My father continued buying me jeans and western shirts, the only shoes I had were cowboy boots, and I'd taken to cutting my own hair just so he wouldn't do it.

Maybe I could've talked to my brothers about it, but were they really that dense? Holt especially, since he knew how bad the taunting had gotten in elementary and middle school.

On the other hand, they had their own issues with our dad, especially since Buck left. His share of our father's bullshit was divided equally among the three remaining boys.

Right after I turned sixteen, Roaring Fork Ranch's cook, Johnny, died of a heart attack while making what he referred to as "morning chow." Since I'd spent so much time with him both when I was told to when I was younger and more recently just because I wanted to, I stepped in to help while my dad looked for another cook.

After three weeks of me handling all three meals every day, I think my dad stopped looking, and consequently, the job became mine—not that he paid me to do it. I didn't mind, though. I loved being in the kitchen, trying out new recipes. It made me especially happy when the cowboys came back for second or third helpings. Suddenly, I was no longer invisible. As they piled food on their plates, they'd occasionally tip their hats and thank me.

I'd get up at four in the morning every day and prep both breakfast and lunch, which some of the ranch hands would help serve on the days I had school. The minute I got home, I'd get dinner going. The downside was, the whole time I cooked, I tasted whatever I was making—and I'd also sit down and eat with my father and brothers.

Being in the kitchen and around food gave me comfort and allowed me to forget, at least for a little while, about the pain of being mercilessly teased every single day. The side effect was I was gaining more weight. It was a vicious cycle.

Most evenings, like tonight, my father and brothers ate in the dining hall with the rest of the hands. I was just about to sit down to join them when my father rushed from the table and hurried outside, covering his mouth with a bandanna.

"His cough is getting worse," I said to Porter.

"Yeah."

"You have to make him go to the doctor."

Cord looked up from his plate. "Did you say *make* him?" Both he and Porter laughed.

I clenched my fists. "I'll do it, then."

Holt looked from our two brothers to me and shook his head.

"Someone has to," I said, staring him down. I knew my three brothers, who were bigger, stronger, and outnumbered my father, were afraid of our "old man," as they called him. I wasn't. What could he or anyone else do to hurt me that would be worse than the pain I'd endured for as long as I could remember?

"I need someone to take me to get my license." I'd been driving since I was ten or eleven. Everyone on the ranch learned how once they could reach the gas pedals. Now that I was sixteen—almost seventeen—I could start doing it legally.

"I'll take you," offered Cord. I'd rather Holt do it, but he didn't speak up. "Maybe we'll get Pops to go with us and dump his ass at the hospital instead." The last part, he'd said under his breath, but I heard him.

* * *

As it turned out, we didn't have to trick our father to get him to go to the hospital; an ambulance delivered him there when Porter found him passed out in the barn.

After running several tests, the doctor came in while I was in the room and gave my father his prognosis. Perhaps if he'd seen a physician sooner, something could have been done to slow the cancer that had spread throughout his body. As it was, my father wasn't expected to live as long as six more months.

"We need to get Buck home," I said to my brothers when I told them what the doctor had said.

"He won't come," said Porter, walking out the front door and slamming it behind him.

"He will," I said to Cord and Holt. "He has to."

7

Irish
Washington, DC
Three Years Ago

"I heard all hell has broken loose in California with Kilbourne's mission," I said to Cope when we met at yet another undisclosed location.

"Things aren't always what they seem."

I studied him, waiting for him to elaborate. It had been three years since Cope let Special Agent Malin Kilbourne run with the mission involving the money that had come into the super PAC and the mystery surrounding the higher-ups and the agency's response.

While he didn't share much, he did occasionally reassure me that she was still very much alive.

"I heard Striker was being airlifted to a hospital." Also in that time, Griffin "Striker" Ellis, once our boss, had left the agency to work for a private intelligence firm called K19 Security Solutions. The man who replaced him at the CIA, Kellen "Money" McTiernan, was the least likely candidate for the job, but he'd been given it anyway.

Rumor was he came by way of the NSA and was known to have an IQ above people like Einstein and Hawking. I hadn't interacted with Money much outside of requisite meetings, and Cope wanted to keep it that way. The fewer people able to track my movement, even during a mission, the better.

"I also heard Ghafor was taken out." The man was the known head of the Islamic State, the organization Kilbourne had been tasked with infiltrating. How she'd lived through that assignment remained a mystery neither Cope nor anyone else could explain.

"Like I said."

"I see." Which meant those on the inside of the mission didn't want anyone in the chain of command to know whatever Kilbourne had unearthed. "So, he's alive."

Cope nodded.

"No ambush."

"That's right."

"McTiernan and I are headed out there now to get a full briefing. Once that's complete, we'll be pulled into a high-level NSA assignment necessitating that we're both off the grid."

So McTiernan was now on the inside. "Who's the target?"

"Montgomery for sure, but we believe it goes way beyond him."

"Stevens?"

"Affirmative."

"Higher?"

"All the way."

"Jesus. Do you think—"

Cope shook his head. "I'd like to believe we were on the cusp of finding out this is connected to our mission, but I don't believe it is, Irish. I can't say it's even related. This is about money, plain and simple."

"Understood."

"I want you to take leave."

Since I was between missions, now was a good time for me to do it.

"I don't want anyone assigning anything to you in my absence. And McTiernan's."

"Does he—"

Cope interrupted me a second time. "No, he is not aware of anything, and I intend to keep it that way as long as possible."

Both Cope and I agreed that until we developed stronger leads, there wasn't anyone we could trust— inside the agency or out.

* * *

The fallout from Malin Kilbourne's mission ended up being widespread and complex. CIA Director James Flatley was dead, the president was facing impeachment and calls for his resignation, and Ed Montgomery was ready to tell everything in order to avoid prosecution—even death—himself. Considering his career spanned several decades, there were as many people anxious about what all he might divulge as he was about doing so. Until he testified, he was buried deep in protective custody.

The more both Cope and I learned, the more we doubted we could draw a line between Kilbourne's mission and our own. Like so many other leads we'd once believed promising, this one fizzled as well.

8

It took a few months, but Buck finally made it home. We'd all worried he wouldn't make it in time. He said he would've come sooner, but he'd been on a mission. Our father didn't believe him, but I did, and I told him so.

Buck cupped my neck with his hand and pulled me into a hug. "You have the sweetest, purest heart of anyone I've ever known, Flynn. Just like our mama did. Don't let life ever change that about you."

He was wrong. If my heart had ever been pure, I feared it no longer was.

So far, my father had outlived his prognosis by over eighteen months, not that the time between then and now was easy. I think it was his fear of death—and spending eternity in hell—that kept him alive. The doctors had offered various types of treatment, most designed to keep him more comfortable, but he'd turned them all down. Which meant he was in almost constant pain. While he might believe he was tough enough to handle it mentally, the physical strain on his body manifested itself in chronic fatigue, periods of incoherence, and ultimately, a seizure so severe that it landed him in the hospital for several days.

The toll it took on me almost landed me there with him.

"You don't have to go see him every day," said Holt when I walked in the house after ten at night.

"If I didn't, no one would."

"You think if one of us was in the hospital, he would give a shit?" asked Cord.

I wasn't going to argue about whether he would or not. That wasn't the point.

Holt walked over and put his arm around my shoulders. "You don't have to be everybody's everything, Flynn. No one expects that of you. Fuck, tell the old man to hire somebody to run the damn dining hall."

His words almost brought me to tears. Working in the dining hall was the one thing I actually liked about my life. If my dad hired somebody, the first thing they'd do is toss me out of there.

I took a deep breath and counted to ten while I let it out. "No."

Holt shrugged and walked away, but Cord looked up from what he was doing. "I know you've had a long day, but there's something I want to talk to you about."

"I'm not—"

"Flynn, it isn't about the old man, and it isn't about hiring a new cook. It's a business idea I want to run by you."

"Yeah? What?"

"I want to turn part of the Roaring Fork into a dude ranch."

"Seriously?" I couldn't contain my smile.

"What do you think?"

"It's an amazing idea."

"We don't have a lot goin' for us right now. We'd need to renovate some of the old cabins and get the North Fork barn fixed up. About the only thing we do have that's working is the food."

"What do you mean?"

"What do you mean what do I mean?"

"What about the food?"

He cocked his head. "It's really fucking good, Flynn."

I felt my cheeks flush, and my eyes opened wide. "Do you think so?"

"Hell, Flynn, everyone thinks so. Word with the cowboys is that the Roaring Fork Ranch has the best food in the valley."

"You're playing with me."

"Hey, Port, get in here."

Our older brother walked around the corner. "What?"

"Which was your favorite dinner this week?"

Porter rubbed his chin. "That's tough. They were all good."

"Yeah, but what's your favorite?"

Porter sat down in one of the living room chairs. "The enchiladas were pretty damn good, but then again, the bison chili was about the best I've ever had."

"The best you ever had?" I said under my breath.

"Shit, Flynn, everything you make is the best I've ever had." Porter studied me. "Why do you look so shocked?"

"You've never said anything."

"That isn't true," both he and Cord said at the same time.

"You're always too busy telling us how if you added this or that ingredient, it would've been better, instead of listening when we tell you how good whatever you made was."

"I don't do that."

Holt came out of his bedroom and leaned his guitar against the wall. "Yeah, you do. You can't take a compliment for shit."

I looked between my three brothers. "I thought you were just being nice."

"Nice? When have you ever known a Wheaton to be nice?" said Porter, messing up my hair. "You're a damn fine cook, Flynn, and Cord is right. That's about all this dude ranch idea has goin' for it."

I really couldn't believe everything my brothers were saying. As much as I tried not to smile, I couldn't help myself.

Cord flipped Porter off, and Holt picked up his guitar and started strumming, while I sat back in my chair, too stunned to get up and go to bed.

"You wanna hear more of my ideas?" asked Cord, sitting down next to me.

"Um, sure."

I tried to listen, but I really wasn't. All I could hear echoing in my head was my brother saying that everything I made was the best he'd ever had.

Cord had been rambling on for about ten minutes when Porter returned and sat down. "Here's the other thing we're thinkin' about." He handed me a piece of paper.

"Roughstock contracting?"

"Yeah, you know, raisin' bulls and broncs for rodeos? Other stuff too."

"Wow."

"You think it's a good idea?"

"I don't know, Port. It sounds like it could be."

"See?" he said to Cord. "It'll work, I'm tellin' you."

Was he telling him because I said it sounded like a good idea? Since when did anyone care what I thought about anything?

"She's tired. You should let her go to bed," said Holt, setting his guitar down. He looked over at Cord. "And if you think this dude ranch idea is a good one, maybe you should get your ass up tomorrow and get in that kitchen and help her."

"I can do that."

When I came out of my bedroom the next morning, Cord was sitting at the dining room table, waiting for me. "Want some coffee?" he asked.

I poured a cup and added cream and sugar to it.

"I've been thinking about buying a smoker. We could do ribs and brisket, maybe even make our own sausage. It could be like our signature thing."

"That sounds really good, Cord."

He beamed at me.

Two hours later, I was on my way to school, feeling more lighthearted than I had maybe in my whole life. So when Janine Nick tried to trip me between first and second period, I hauled off and punched her in the gut.

Mrs. Mancuso saw the whole thing too, yet when Janine asked if she was going to write me up and send me to the office, our science teacher told her the only thing she saw was Janine trying to trip me.

They might call me a heifer, but Janine and everyone else would soon learn that I had the strength of a god-damn bull.

9

Irish

Washington, DC, to New York, New York

Two Years Ago

When I almost lost my life a third time, in an inexplicable ambush—the second of its kind that took place in Beijing—both Cope and I decided we needed to step up our efforts.

"There's a mole," I said. "Someone is feeding information to the Chinese government, and it's getting agents killed."

"By someone, do you mean inside the agency?"

"Yes."

"I agree."

"It's someone high up, Cope."

"I believe it is."

"Within the agency, or do you think it's broader than that?" After Agent Kilbourne's mission ended with a dead CIA director and a number of high-ranking government officials either in prison or on their way there, I wouldn't rule anything out.

"Broader, definitely. I'm going to ask you something outright, and I'll warn you, you aren't going to like it."

"What?"

"Are you absolutely certain you want to continue this mission?"

I was incredulous. How could he even ask?

"I know what you're thinking."

"You do? So why'd you bother?"

Cope stood, grabbed a bottle of whiskey, and handed it to me. "Because it's you risking your life, Irish. I sit behind a desk."

"If someone finds out about our investigation, do you think I'd be the only one they kill?"

"No, but—"

"There's your answer. It's your neck too, Cope. You want to back out, go right ahead. I'll continue with or without you."

Two days later, Cope asked that we meet at one of our off-site locations. When I sat down at the bistro table across from him, he handed me an envelope.

"Dr. Emerson Charles. Research analyst and political strategist with MIT's International Policy Program." I looked up at him. "What about her?"

"One of the world's foremost experts on China."

I kept reading. The stated objective was to recruit the doctor as a CIA asset. The reason the agency was fast-tracking the mission was because MI6 had expressed an interest in doing the same.

"Do you know who they're sending in?" I asked.

"Saint."

I rolled my eyes. It was sometimes hard to believe Niven St. Thomas, code name Saint, was still employed by any intelligence agency, let alone SIS. Word was, he was the least effective operative with MI6, unless the qualifier was bedding women. In that case, rumor was he was a pro.

As I finished reading the brief on Dr. Charles' background, I couldn't help but grow more curious about MI6's choice of Saint. What I read indicated the woman's intelligence quotient was well above genius level. The photos of her in the file weren't unattractive. She was no beauty queen-type, but something told me she would see right through seduction.

"I have approval to send you in with a stated objective of asset acquisition. Your cover is research assistant to Dr. Charles. You will have access to every point of information she has amassed on China in every conceivable category, whether political, economic, or militaristic."

"When do I start?"

"Two weeks."

* * *

I'd been at MIT, working with Dr. Charles, for over eight months when Cope scheduled an urgent meeting. Since it was a holiday weekend, I offered to come to DC. Instead, we settled on New York City and agreed to meet at Frankie and Johnnie's Steakhouse on Thirty-seventh.

Over two T-bones, Cope read me in on a man named Adam Benjamin.

"Officially, he's a British diplomat. He's also an MI6 asset. If you think Dr. Charles has strong opinions in regard to China, this guy has her beat by a mile. Especially when it comes to Hong Kong."

I thumbed through Benjamin's file. As a world-renowned expert on China, he'd been the first to suggest MI6 recruit Emme as an asset, believing that in her, he'd found a comrade in arms. With him as a policy influencer for the UK and her a policy writer for the US, they'd make a formidable team. They were equally impassioned about the threat China posed not just to our two countries, but to the world.

I knew, from the many conversations she and I had had, what loomed great in her mind was the idea that China had become a "systemic rival" to the world's superpowers, one whose economic power and political influence had grown with unprecedented scale and speed.

What I hadn't been able to share with her but weighed just as heavily deep in my soul, was their apparent systematic annihilation of some of the best agents and operatives in the intelligence world.

"Benjamin has requested a meeting with Dr. Charles later this week. Be sure to sit in on it."

"That ought to be mind-numbingly exciting."

He chuckled. "Try not to nod off."

It felt good to laugh, even if it was fleeting. This mission had taken most of the joy out of both of our lives. Even when I was on another mission, I was thinking about this one. I occasionally went out to bars, but the conversations I got into with women either depressed or frustrated me. While there was a possibility they led lives more interesting than their stories indicated, I hadn't met one yet that produced a spark.

In bars, that was. I felt sparks on a daily basis, but with the one woman I knew I shouldn't think about that way—Dr. Charles. Being around Emme, as she insisted I call her, was like spending every day basking in the heat of the sun.

The woman was brilliant, of course, but with quirks I found beguiling. I smiled more when I was in her presence than I had since before I was recruited by the agency. Even Cope had noticed the change in my demeanor.

"Don't get attached," he warned me when we walked out of the restaurant's elevator and out onto the bustling streets of New York.

"What are you talking about?"

"Dr. Charles."

While I scowled at him, I heeded his warning. As much as Emme intrigued me, I knew he was right.

10

Irish
Cambridge, Massachusetts
August of the Preceding Year

I left the meeting with Emme and Dr. Benjamin feeling unsettled. There was something about the man that didn't add up for me. Every instinct told me to proceed with caution in a way that was illogical, particularly given the man's appearance.

A single word could be used to describe him—disheveled. His hair, his clothes, even his shoes looked as though they were long beyond their useful life. The glasses he wore were held together by yellowed tape, his dress shirt was wrinkled, and there appeared to be a stain on the sweater he likely wore seven days a week.

His attire wouldn't be the focus of the brief I'd give Cope once our meeting concluded, though. Instead, it would be about what could only be described as his obsession with the conflict between Hong Kong and China.

I'd read his dossier; the man had never lived in Hong Kong, didn't have family members who did, and according to MI6, spent only occasional time there. Yet his passions equated those of someone whose family had lived there for several generations. He spoke of the huge protest marches and street battles, where Chinese police responded with tear gas, rubber bullets, water cannons, and live fire, with what felt to me like an inappropriate level of emotional intensity.

I sensed Emme's similar discomfort as she attempted several times to bring the conversation back around to what she believed to be the main reason for the meeting—China as it related to the rest of the world, not just Hong Kong. When that seemed impossible, she asked me how much time we had left before our next meeting that afternoon. While we didn't have any others scheduled, I told her we'd need to wrap things up within fifteen minutes or we'd be late.

After walking Dr. Benjamin out of the building, I went to the parking garage and called Cope.

"The guy is borderline certifiable," I told him.

"In what way?"

I explained the extremity of the man's views and that I was certain Emme had picked up on it as well.

"You should get Saint's take on it," he suggested.

As much as I didn't want to engage the MI6 agent, I knew Cope was right.

The meeting between Saint and me lasted all of ten minutes. It took longer to order our beer at the bar we'd agreed to meet at than to get his response to my questions about Dr. Benjamin.

"He's harmless," said Saint, taking a sip of his pint. "One would think a CIA agent would have the proper intuition to make that determination."

I finished my beer and walked out before I gave in to the temptation to throat punch him.

I hadn't been at my apartment long when Cope called me.

"We have a problem with Dr. Benjamin."

Given my reaction to the man, Cope's news came as no surprise. "What?"

"He made contact with McTiernan to alert him of a potential mole at MIT—in international policy. Someone he believes, as we do, is feeding information to the Chinese."

That surprised me. Someone I hadn't found suspicious myself? How was this a problem? "At MIT?"

"No guesses?"

I took a deep breath. There were times Cope reminded me of a child.

"Nobody?"

"Get to the fucking point, Copeland."

"You."

"You're kidding."

His tone changed from playful to serious. "No. I'm not."

"Interesting."

"Tell me what you're thinking."

"We use this to our advantage."

"How so?" he asked.

"Keeping the heat on me might give the real mole a false sense of being in the clear."

"How do you want to proceed?"

"Stay the course, Cope."

It had been a week since the meeting between Dr. Benjamin, Emme, and me, along with the call from Cope about the man's suspicions that I was a mole. I couldn't shake the feeling that I knew him from somewhere. He looked so damned familiar, and yet I couldn't place him. I'd spent hours scouring for every image of him I could find, and still, nothing registered.

Close to dawn, I bolted up in bed, drenched in sweat, realizing, perhaps in a dream, where I recognized him from. He'd been one of the men on the street corner in Hong Kong that night when Dingo, 337, and Julius were gunned down.

"There's something I need to tell you about Dr. Benjamin," I said to Cope when I called him at a little after six in the morning.

"I already know." He sounded as though he'd been up for hours.

"You do? How?"

"I got a call from Money McTiernan."

It dawned on me that even though Cope and I were talking about the same man, it was about different subjects.

"What did McTiernan tell you?" I asked.

"Benjamin's and Saint's last known whereabouts were in Hong Kong. They've both been missing for five days. Zero contact."

"No shit?" I muttered, not intending to say it out loud.

"What were you going to tell me?"

"I realized where I recognized him from. That night, also in Hong Kong, I'd swear he was one of the men I saw standing on the street corner. Remember? I told you about them."

"No shit?" Cope repeated. "Are you certain?"

"Not one hundred percent but damn near. The man has a very distinctive look." It wasn't as though I could see details from a distance that night. It was more the way he carried himself.

"Are you thinking what I'm thinking?" he asked.

"When am I not?"

"Best way to remove attention from yourself is to point it in someone else's direction."

"You said Saint is missing as well."

"He accompanied the doctor to Hong Kong."

"Were you aware he intended to?" I asked.

"I was not."

* * *

"Good morning, Emme," I said a few days later, before turning to Lynx, the man I'd been alerted was being sent in by MI6 to lead the search for Saint and Dr. Benjamin. "This must be Mr. Edgemon. I'm Paxon Warrick." I held out my hand, and he shook it.

"Emerson," I heard him say, wondering why he mumbled a name she rarely used.

"Yes?" she asked.

"Do you need a few moments before our meeting?"

"Um...sure," she answered. "How did you know my...never mind. I'm sure it was in Dr. Benjamin's notes." My guess was she was about to ask how he knew her first name was actually Emerson, but decided against it.

"I'll show our guest to the conference room," I offered.

"Wait. Were you aware we were meeting with Mr. Edgemon instead of Dr. Benjamin?" she asked me.

"I was."

Emme looked puzzled, and I wondered if she'd asked why I hadn't shared that information with her.

"I received an email. I assumed you did too," I said, hoping that would be enough of an explanation.

"Hmm," she murmured, picking up her bags and walking in the direction of her office.

"Follow me," I said to Lynx when Emme disappeared down the hallway. "Coffee? No, wait. You're a tea drinker."

"Neither, thanks. Water would be nice, though."

I led him into the conference room. "I'll forewarn you that Emme—Dr. Charles—can be...quirky, and that's an understatement. But she's a brilliant analyst." While I was on a first-name basis with her, the idea that Lynx would eventually be as well, rankled. I'd do nothing to encourage it.

"As well as strategist."

I grabbed an envelope from the other side of the table and slid it in Lynx's direction. "Beautiful too," I mumbled, wishing I hadn't as soon as I said it. My feelings for Emme were proprietary, given we'd worked so closely together over the past few months. I had to remind myself—again—that I was undercover and whatever I felt for her was inappropriate.

"How close are the two of you?" he asked.

I couldn't help but be curious why he would want to know. The question seemed as inappropriate as my own feelings. I wondered if there was something more between them than either was letting on. I decided to press harder to gauge his reaction.

"Not as close as I'd like, but after this mission is over, who knows?" I wasn't surprised when that appeared to have pissed him off.

"She hasn't given the impression that she knows anything about Saint's disappearance," I said quietly when I returned with his glass of water. "Or Dr. Benjamin's."

"That was evident."

"How so?"

"We crossed paths at their apartment building."

"What did she say?"

"Nothing specific, only that her demeanor when I mentioned knowing Niven was one of curiosity rather than concern."

"Serendipitous, meeting her," I commented.

"Or not."

"Have a seat." I motioned to a chair.

"I'll wait for Dr. Charles. In fact, I'd prefer to meet with her alone."

What the fuck was this guy up to? "Why? She expects me to be in the meeting."

"I'm sure you'll think of some reason you're unable to join us."

"Let me know when you'd like to debrief." I walked out of the room and headed straight to call Cope.

"I don't trust this guy," I told him, giving him the rundown of what had happened so far this morning.

"His behavior does seem odd."

"Maybe he's the mole."

Cope was silent.

"I especially don't trust him with Dr. Charles."

"Keep close watch, and in the meantime, I'll see if I can find more information on Edgemon."

"Roger that."

Fifteen minutes later, I found Emme and Lynx in the lobby, blood pouring from a gash in her scalp.

"What happened?" I gasped. I looked from Emme to Lynx, whose pants appeared to be drenched.

"A little accident. I spilled water, and then things just got…worse," she answered, trying to get around me.

I put my hand on her arm and led her over to a chair in the lobby. "Sit there and don't move." I turned to Lynx. "She has a first aid kit in her office."

"Yes," he said, pointing to something Emme held in her hand.

"What's that?" I asked.

"It's a liquid bandage. If you'd just put some on my cut, it will stop the bleeding," she said, trying to hand it to me.

"Is she kidding?" I asked Lynx.

"I'm afraid she's somewhat intransigent."

"Let me have a look." I moved her hand and lifted the sopping paper towels. "It's bleeding a lot and looks to be about five centimeters. I'm sorry, Emme, but you're going to have to go to the emergency room."

"*No!*" she shrieked, startling me. "No hospitals."

When Lynx nudged me out of the way and knelt in front of her, I wanted to belt him. However, Emme's head was bleeding profusely and needed immediate attention. If he could convince her to get medical care, I'd step aside.

"The laceration is this long," he said, spreading his fingers. "Your desired treatment won't stop the bleeding. You need to see a doctor."

I pulled out my phone and checked the schedule for the on-campus clinic. "Medical services is closed until two," I said. "What about Cambridge Urgent Care?"

"I've another idea. Give me a moment?" said Lynx.

We both watched as he pulled out his phone and made a call.

"Emerson, where is building 14?" he asked a couple of minutes later.

"Right behind that building there," I answered for her.

"Is it where the medical services are located?"

"Yes, but—"

The bastard held up his hand as if to silence me. Before I realized what was happening, he was escorting her from the building.

"Wait. Will you be okay?" I walked over and squeezed her shoulder.

"I'll be with her," Lynx snapped.

"Right. Well, I'll be in the office later if you need anything," I said, although it didn't appear either heard me.

Hours later, I had no idea where either Lynx or Emme had gone, other than to the clinic, which was closed, when I got a call from Cope.

"I've received word that before he disappeared, Saint managed a brush pass with one of our agents."

The term referred to one operative essentially "brushing past" another in order to hand off some kind of physical item, most often a coded message. "What did it say?"

"First of all, he confirmed tracking Dr. Benjamin to Hong Kong. Second, and I'm quoting, 'We don't protect them because they are weak. We protect them because they are strong, and strong people make enemies.'"

"He has to be referring to Dr. Charles."

"Or Dr. Benjamin."

"Doubtful, but okay. Was that the extent of it?"

"Affirmative. Do you want to relay this information to Edgemon?"

"Roger that." I didn't want to tell Cope how long it had been since I knew where he and Emme were. If they didn't surface in the next hour, I'd alert him.

It was almost ten at night when Lynx pulled up to Emme's building, where I'd been waiting for the last few hours. I walked over and opened the passenger door. After helping Emme out, I stuck my head back in the car. "Where have you been?"

"Dinner, not that it's any of your business," he spat.

"We need to talk."

"She knows who I am," he said, motioning to where Dr. Charles waited just inside the foyer.

"About Saint," I spat back, slamming the door and stalking away. As livid as I was, I knew better than to let Emme see any more of my anger than she already had. Why had he divulged his identity to her? It made no sense.

Like earlier, I called Cope and told him what Lynx had said.

"What the fuck is he up to?"

"My question precisely."

"I'll follow up with Z about this, but, Irish, I suggest you be proactive with your own cover story before she digs any deeper. Regardless of what Lynx may have told her, stick to the story that the CIA put you in place in order to gain her as an asset."

"What about Saint and Benjamin?"

"Since the CIA received the message, it makes perfect sense you would be read in on it. It also makes sense you, in turn, would read Lynx in."

"Roger that."

"I don't need to tell you what it will mean for both of us if Dr. Charles figures out what you're really doing undercover at MIT."

"Understood."

"You need to sell this and sell it good, Irish."

After ending my call with Cope, I went up to Saint's apartment where Lynx was staying. I read him in on the brush pass but cut him off when he began asking questions. "I need to speak with Dr. Charles." I heard him ask why as I walked out, but I ignored him, walked over to her apartment, and knocked.

"Can I come in?" I asked when she pulled it open.

"Of course," she said, waving me in. I noticed her look beyond me.

"He's not with me. I asked for a few minutes on my own."

"Okay. Can I get you anything?"

"No. I'm here to apologize."

"There's nothing to apologize for. You're doing your job."

"Sometimes, the hardest part of being undercover is getting to know the people you work with and then feeling regret that the role you play in their lives isn't real."

"I understand. What happens now?"

"Nothing changes, except that you know who I really am, and that makes it harder on you. On the other hand, both Lynx and I are going to ask you to help us, and that we can be upfront about it, makes it easier for everyone."

"Does anyone else know who you really are?"

"Only Dr. Baker." The man was the head of the International Policy Program, so it had been necessary for Dr. Baker to approve us working undercover within IPP's walls.

"Are you going to tell me what's happening with Saint, or is Lynx?"

"He will."

"Thank you for coming over to talk to me rather than waiting until tomorrow when it might be awkward."

"It's late. I should go." She seemed accepting of what I considered a vague explanation. Giving her the chance to ask me more questions would compromise my real mission. Lynx's mission was exactly what she believed both of ours to be—finding the British diplomat and the wayward MI6 agent that had been put on the man's detail. I wouldn't be the slightest bit surprised if we ultimately learned the two missing men were double agents.

Emme walked me to the door, but before I could walk out, she put her hand on my shoulder. When I turned, she hugged me. The relief I felt at her gesture was a reminder that I'd allowed myself to care far too much about her.

"I'll talk to you later," I said, stepping out into the hallway. Instead of going back to Saint's apartment, I waited for the elevator. The doors had just opened when Lynx brushed past me without a word.

I was walking through the lobby when I received another call from Cope.

"I've just ended calls with both Lynx and Z."

Archer "Z" Alexander was the head of MI6, and thus Lynx and Saint's boss.

"What happens next is Z's call since it's an MI6 agent and a British diplomat who are missing. He's decided to bring in a third-party private intelligence firm to locate them."

"Which firm?"

"They're new. They call themselves the Invincibles Intelligence and Security Group."

"I heard Decker Ashford joined up with them." The man was an enigma and a genius when it came to intelligence technology. There wasn't a single person in the business who hadn't heard of him.

"He hasn't made it official yet," said Cope. "But if he's brought in on this mission, it may not bode well for our investigation."

"What do you mean?" I asked.

"The guy doesn't miss much."

"I'll just have to keep a low profile."

"I'm thinking you should play up your infatuation with Dr. Charles. That way, if you seem too attentive, that explanation would be readily accepted."

"Roger that," I said, wondering which of the agents working this op Cope believed were the type to readily accept anything.

I ended the call and went across the street and a few doors down to a bar that had outdoor seating. I wasn't there long before I saw Lynx walk up. The man looked as bone-tired as I was.

"You look like I feel," I said, raising my pint to him. He waved and went in the bar's main entrance. A few minutes later, he came out with a pint and a shot.

"I didn't expect to see you again tonight," I said when he pulled out a chair and sat down.

"Nor I, you."

I decided to do as Cope suggested and play up my interest in Dr. Charles. "I guess I know why you asked how close Emme and I are this morning."

"It isn't what you think."

I shook my head. "I said I'd like our relationship to change once the mission was over. You decided not to wait."

"We've met once before."

His tone explained a great deal; I didn't need to ask any further questions about their "personal" relationship.

"Have you come to any decisions about who to use for Saint and Dr. Benjamin's extraction?" I asked as though I didn't already know.

"Yes. A private firm."

"Who's heading it up?"

"Decker Ashford and Cortez DeLéon."

"Rile?"

"Yes."

Rile DeLéon had a long career as an MI6 agent as well as ties to both the British and Spanish monarchies. "I heard they started a new group. Some bullshit name like the Invincibles or something."

He laughed. "That is correct."

"What's the plan?" I asked just as his cell rang.

"This is Decker now." His call was brief, and when it ended, he told me the Invincibles team would be arriving in the morning.

I took another drink of my beer. "About Emme—"

"She was seeing Saint."

I hadn't seen that coming. "No shit?"

Lynx didn't respond.

"How much does she know?" I asked.

"Only that there was a brush pass, but not the details of it."

I drained the rest of the beer from my glass and set it on the table. "Early start tomorrow," I said, tossing some money on the table and hopping the fence to leave.

Lynx called a meeting for zero eight hundred the next morning, oddly at Emme's apartment rather than at Saint's.

"What are you doing here?" she asked when she responded to my knock at her door. "Sorry," she added when she saw I brought her coffee and bagels from her favorite place. I looked around when she invited me in; I was obviously the first to arrive.

"Lynx is on his way over, too," I said, just now noticing she was clad in only a robe. She must've realized it at the exact moment I did since she scurried down the hall.

"Give me a minute. Make yourself at home," she hollered behind her.

While I waited for her to change, Decker Ashford arrived.

"Hello. Who are you?" Emme said to him a few minutes later when she came back into the kitchen.

"I'm Decker Ashford, ma'am," he said, stepping forward to shake her hand.

"Emerson Charles," she responded, looking at me although I had no idea why. "I'm sorry, I know you told me your name, but why are you in my apartment?"

Evidently, she hadn't been briefed on this meeting or that it was taking place here. Damn Lynx. "Decker is part of a team we're working with to locate Saint and Dr. Benjamin," I told her at the same time there was another knock at her door.

"Would you like to get that?" she snapped.

"Uh, sure."

When I opened the door, Lynx walked in.

"I would offer you gentlemen something; however, I was unaware a meeting was taking place in *my home* this morning." Emme glared at me as she said it, only pissing me off more at Lynx.

"You didn't make Dr. Charles aware of the meeting?" I finally asked, getting tired of Emme taking her anger out on me.

"I called, but it went straight to voicemail," he said to her.

"Are we expecting anyone else?" she asked.

"No, and let's take this over to Saint's apartment," Lynx suggested before I had the chance to.

"I'm curious why you didn't meet there in the first place."

I looked at Lynx, expecting him to answer, but he didn't. I motioned Decker to the door, expecting Lynx to follow. He didn't do that either.

Several minutes later, he and Emme walked into Saint's apartment together. I watched as he introduced her to the other men in the room from the Invincibles: Rile, Miles "Grinder" Stone, and Lynx's younger brother, Keon "Edge" Edgemon. Both Grinder and Edge had formerly been employed by the MI5 side of SIS, aka Her Majesty's Secret Intelligence Service, which was akin to the US Department of Homeland Security.

"Are we ready to get down to business?" asked Decker once the introductions concluded.

I took the lead. "Emme, as you're aware, the CIA and MI6 have been working jointly undercover at IPP the last few months."

She appeared to be listening but walked over to the window, keeping her back to us.

I continued. "These gentlemen were asked to come on board after the CIA received word of a brush pass between one of our agents and Saint." I took a step closer to her. "They're with a private security and intelligence firm who will be leading the mission from this point on."

Emme tapped her lips with her fingertip. "What was the mission?"

"To locate Saint and Dr. Benjamin," I answered.

"That isn't what I asked. I said, 'What was the mission?' Not what is the mission."

I looked at Lynx, who shook his head. If I didn't believe we were close to uncovering information that might give us our first real lead about the mole who was feeding the Chinese information about agents who in turn were dying, I'd walk out.

"Maybe we should consider working from a remote field office rather than at MIT," I suggested, given Saint's odd message.

"A remote location? Where? Or is that another question you're refusing to answer?"

Refusing to answer? What the fuck was that all about? "The Boston CIA field office."

She looked between Lynx and me. "Gentlemen, until you are prepared to be completely honest with me, there's nothing further for us to discuss."

I stepped closer. "Emme, you're a target."

"What does that mean?"

"What do you think it means?" Hadn't Lynx covered any of this with her?

"Are you saying you believe I'm in danger?"

I really wished we didn't have an audience. "I'm sorry, but I do, Emme. Now you understand why I'm suggesting we work from the field office."

"I want my apartment swept."

I hadn't heard that her apartment or even the building had been compromised. "Do you think that's necessary?"

"Yes. It's necessary," said Lynx, evidently no longer mute. "She also needs a keypad entry installed."

"We'll take care of both," said Decker, motioning to Grinder and Edge.

Emme walked toward the door. "If you don't need me for anything else right now..."

"I'll walk you over," Lynx offered.

When they both left, I breathed a sigh of relief. I'd worked with Emme—Dr. Charles—for several months and recognized the signs when she was getting agitated.

Had we been alone, I might've been able to diffuse her increasing ire. As it was, she probably felt as though we were ganging up on her.

"Come with me," said Decker, motioning for me to follow him to one of the bedrooms he'd set up as his office. "You wanna tell me what the fuck is really going on?" he asked after shutting the door behind us.

I walked over to the window and looked outside. "We need to bring Cope in on this."

Decker studied me.

"I can make contact or you can, but this isn't a conversation I can have without him present."

Deck nodded. "It sounds like Lynx is back. Hang on," he said, going out to the other room.

"He's gone again," he said when he returned a couple of minutes later, closed the door like he had earlier, and pulled out his phone.

"What are you doing?"

"Calling Cope."

"We can't discuss this over the phone."

Decker raised a brow, and I stopped talking. If anyone could guarantee the conversation we were about to have wouldn't be overheard either outside the walls of this room or over a phone line, it was him.

11

Irish

Cambridge, Massachusetts

August of the Preceding Year

I couldn't say why Cope and I trusted Decker with a yearslong mission that only he and I knew about, but we did. Maybe we'd both just reached the point when we knew we couldn't go it alone any longer.

I reiterated most of what had happened in the last seven years in terms of my tracking the inexplicable deaths of agents, primarily in Hong Kong and China, but also elsewhere around the world.

The fact that he continued making notes on a second computer should've alarmed me. Oddly, it didn't.

"Tell me more about the number of deaths and the span of time."

"I haven't tabulated in the same way I did in the past since I arrived in Boston."

"Understood."

A few minutes later, Decker turned his laptop around so both Cope and I could see the screen. What he showed me made my eyes bug out. In just a few minutes, he'd compiled the same data I had, including the deaths and where they'd taken place. Sadly, the total number was nearing the hundred mark.

Decker sat back in his chair and remained silent for several minutes.

"There's another thing you need to be aware of," said Cope.

Decker sighed. "Go ahead."

"Shortly after first meeting with Irish and Dr. Charles, Dr. Benjamin contacted McTiernan directly to suggest that Irish was a mole. Somehow, Fisk got wind of it. Since, the director has been snooping around in a way that's making me uncomfortable."

"Are you saying the director of the CIA is snooping around *personally*?" Decker asked, looking from me to Cope.

"Affirmative."

"In that case, we need to find something before he does."

"Meaning?" I asked.

"Proof that you are, in fact, the mole."

"Then what?"

"We start by creating enough evidence that will result in your carefully planned arrest, by which we accomplish two things. First, we make arrangements for you to be incarcerated where we can protect you.

Second, the easiest way to get a mole to dig in deeper is to make him or her believe someone has taken the fall for them."

Before Decker could continue, his cell rang. "Excuse me." He left the room, but returned seconds later. "Gentlemen, our job just got a hell of a lot easier."

"In what way?" asked Cope.

"I've enlisted the help of Buster Stevens. The next step will be to arrange a meeting between him, Matrix, and Lynx. Of course, we'll need to make sure Matrix believes the whole thing was his idea."

Cope's blank expression mirrored mine.

"Matrix is Dr. Charles' father, and I'm sure you know who Buster is."

"US Ambassador to China."

"Wait," said Cope. "*Matrix* is Emme's father?"

Decker either didn't feel the need to respond or he hadn't heard Cope's question. "The next step is to plant the evidence and lead either the doctor or her father to it."

"What happens after that?" I asked.

"You're arrested."

"Back up a little bit. You said Lynx is meeting with the ambassador. What's the agenda for that meeting?" asked Cope.

"They'll make arrangements for Buster to help facilitate Dr. Benjamin and Saint's release. In the meantime, I'll work on planting evidence."

"You've confirmed they're being detained?" I asked.

Decker raised a brow but, like before, didn't respond. "There's something else I need to make you aware of."

"Okay."

"We have reason to believe Lynx and our Dr. Charles may have history."

"They do. He admitted it to me. He also said she was involved with Saint."

"I don't think so. However, I do believe there may be an advantage to him thinking you're interested as well."

"I've already said as much."

"What about Dr. Charles? Does she believe you have an interest in more than a professional relationship with her?"

"I don't believe so."

"Again, it may work in our favor if she did."

Decker got an alert on his phone. "Speaking of Dr. Charles, it appears she's leaving. Warrick, go and see if you can find out where she's headed."

"Going somewhere?" I asked, eyeing Emme's suitcase near the door.

"To see my parents."

"When will you be back?"

"I'm not sure, Paxon."

"Can I give you a lift?"

"No, um, Lynx's driver is taking me."

"Huh. Okay, well, can I walk you downstairs?"

She thanked me and walked into the waiting elevator; I followed. Once inside, I set the bag down that I'd been carrying for her. I wanted to warn her about my suspicions that Lynx was a mole, but that was part of a mission she knew nothing about—and never could. Instead, I went with Decker's suggestion.

"Emme...I...um...just want you to know...Lynx told me about you and Saint."

"Yes, well..." she stammered.

I cleared my throat and took a step closer. "I realize this might be coming out of left field for you, but to be honest, once this mission was over, I planned to ask you out myself."

Evidently, my proclamation left her speechless. Something I hadn't seen very often.

"Uh, that's very nice..." she said as we exited the elevator.

I handed Emme's bag to the driver and put my hand on her arm. "Wait. I want you to know that when this guy's boss leaves your heart in pieces"—I pointed to the driver—"there's someone who cares enough to help you put it back together."

She got in the car without another word, and they sped off.

"Any luck?" Deck asked when I returned to the apartment's bedroom.

"She's headed down the Cape to her parents' place. I was also able to suggest that if things don't work out with Lynx, I'd be waiting in the wings."

"Excellent on both fronts. As for her visiting her parents, the longer she stays there, the better for us. Excuse me for a moment," he said, standing and leaving the room.

"How are you feeling about this?" Cope asked after the door closed.

"Not sure."

"Understood."

"Do you trust Ashford?"

"Kind of late to ask, Irish."

"I mean moving forward."

"I'd rather you not be arrested. However, with Decker's involvement, we have access to support we haven't had to this point."

"Backup?" I asked.

"Exactly. Decker said he'd make arrangements for you to be held in a place where we can keep you safe. That means he intends to have people on the inside."

After ending the video conference, I heard Decker's raised voice in the hallway. "Lynx, are you aware Dr. Charles is on her way out of town?" There were a few seconds of silence. "Where are you now?" he asked as I eased the door open.

Decker ended the call and set the phone down. "He's on his way back here."

A few minutes later, when we heard the code being entered into the keypad, Decker motioned for me to go into the bedroom. "Ready to do this?" he asked.

"Affirmative."

A few seconds later, he came in with Lynx.

"No one knew Dr. Charles was leaving?" Deck asked me.

I pointed at Lynx. "*His* driver took her."

"Took her where?" Lynx asked.

"To visit her parents."

"You didn't know about this?" Decker asked him.

"Of course I didn't." Lynx pulled out his phone and placed a call.

"He's your driver; how did you not know?" I asked.

"Tell me what he looked like."

"The driver?"

After I'd described him, Lynx placed another call. "I need transport arranged from Boston to Cape Cod." He ended the call.

"What's your plan?" Deck asked.

"I'd like to wring her neck before we return."

"You might not want to bring Emerson back right away."

Bingo. That was the setup Deck, Cope, and I had discussed. In order to have enough time to plant evidence suggesting I was the mole—or double agent—we needed her to stay away from MIT for several days, at least.

"Why not?"

I watched Decker hand Lynx an envelope, the contents of which I'd already read.

"What's this?"

"Background on Emerson's father."

I was sure Decker shared my hope that learning about Matrix would distract Lynx from asking any more questions about why Emme needed to be kept away from her office.

"Thanks for this," Lynx said after reading through it.

"I'll brief you on what else we know as we know it."

"My transport is waiting," he said, walking into the main room to say goodbye to the three other men in the apartment, all of whom were on their laptops.

After Lynx said goodbye to Rile, Grinder, and Edge, he walked toward the front door. I followed.

"I hardly need an escort," he snapped as I continued to follow him to the elevator.

"I'm going with you."

"You're doing nothing of the kind."

"This is the CIA's mission as much as it is yours."

"The CIA's initial mission was to convert Dr. Charles into an asset in the same way MI6 intended to. Given that the mission was aborted upon the disappearance of one of our assets along with one of our agents, you are no longer needed." The elevator door closed between us.

"How'd it go?" asked Deck when I came back into the bedroom.

I looked over my shoulder to make sure Edge wasn't paying attention. "As planned."

Decker and I spent the next two days in my office at MIT, pulling reports designed to make it look as though I was stockpiling information.

Mid-afternoon on the second day, my cell rang with a call from Emme. Decker motioned for me to take it. I put the call on speaker.

"Paxon, I'd like to make arrangements to return to Boston."

Decker shook his head.

"You can't," I said.

"What do you mean I can't?"

"What did Lynx tell you about the brush pass?"

"Paxon, I am in no mood for games. If there's something I need to know, just…fucking…*tell me!*"

"Okay, you don't have to yell. Saint's message contained a warning."

"What…was…the…warning?"

"Essentially, it said to keep you safe."

"That isn't a warning."

"Look, you need to talk to Lynx. If you don't want to talk to him, talk to your dad."

"*My dad? What the hell does my dad have to do with this?*" she shouted. "Are you going to answer me?" she said when I didn't respond.

"I can't. Talk to Lynx." I ended the call when Decker indicated I should.

"Good work," he said. "The next step is to make Lynx believe we're running surveillance on you."

I continued going to my office at MIT for several more days, each time tailed by either Edge, Grinder, or Rile.

"I want you to stick around here today," Decker said, showing up at my apartment as I was getting ready to leave for Cambridge.

"What's going on?"

"Matrix is in the city, and I've asked him to get Lynx and Dr. Charles back here."

"This is it, then." The plan was that once Emme returned from the Cape, Decker would set the stage for her to stumble on the evidence suggesting I was selling secrets to the Chinese.

"I'm also hearing chatter coming out of Beijing."

"What kind of chatter?"

"My sources say an announcement is going to be made today regarding Saint and Dr. Benjamin."

"Do you think they're alive?"

"I haven't heard otherwise." He took a small earpiece out of his laptop bag and handed it to me.

"What's this?"

"Ears."

"What do you mean?"

He sighed in the same way he often did when I asked a question about something he thought I should already know or understand. "I'll signal you when we're ready to set up the arrest. In the meantime, you'll be able to follow along."

I listened over the course of the next few hours as several things happened.

First, Decker sent me a message saying he'd been successful in replacing the reports Emme had taken with her to the Cape with the ones that held the code that would "prove" I was the mole. With that done, all that was left was furthering the setup of my arrest with Lynx, Emme, and her father.

"We have reason to believe Paxon Warrick has been gathering intelligence that he is selling to the Chinese," I heard him say a few minutes later through the earpiece.

"He's a double agent?" Emme asked.

"We believe so," Decker answered.

"Lynx said this involves me somehow."

"We need to be certain," a voice that sounded like her father said. "In order for that to happen, we need you to return to your office."

"To feed him specific information?" she asked.

This was news to me, and I didn't like it. There was no reason Emme needed to be anywhere near MIT when my arrest took place.

"That's right," said the voice I assumed was her father. "Emme, you should know Lynx is not in favor of this."

"Why not?"

"In order for this to work, the two of you will need to be alone," I heard Lynx's voice for the first time.

"We worked alone for weeks."

The next thing I heard were several alerts going off on cell phones, including my own.

I walked over and turned on the television when I heard Decker say there was a press conference taking place.

The ticker on the bottom of the screen said, "*Breaking News/Special Report,*" and the headline at the top of the screen read, "Two Americans and two Brits arrested in China, sentenced to death on drug-trafficking charges." There, on the dais to the side of the podium where a Chinese official stood, were Dr. Adam Benjamin and Niven St. Thomas. Next to them stood two other men—both I recognized as CIA agents I'd worked with on past missions.

I continued to listen as Decker made arrangements for a team to immediately mobilize to Beijing. He would not be part of that team as originally planned since he was needed here to facilitate my arrest.

Lynx, Rile, Grinder, and Edge were set to be dispatched to China along with Buster Stevens. The ambassador would be accompanying them under the auspice of further negotiation, rather than the planned extraction. Buster's job would be to insist he and the UK ambassador meet with the prisoners to confirm their health and well-being before making the deal to meet the Chinese demands. By the end of that meeting, the Invincibles team would have the prisoners' extraction set up and ready to execute.

I'd seen missions like this happen dozens of times. I just prayed that whoever the real mole was, wasn't privy to the details of the op and that the agents involved all made it out alive.

I was making myself dinner when I received another text from Decker, alerting me of a meeting he was about to have with Emme and her father.

"Decker, do you want to fill Emme in on what you've uncovered?" I heard Matrix say.

"As you know, US intelligence—the CIA specifically—has suffered major setbacks in China. The agency has been convinced there was a mole feeding information to Chinese intelligence officers," Deck told her.

"And you suspect Paxon?"

"More than suspect, Emme," said her father.

"While it wasn't his original mission, Saint was also investigating Irish, based on information he was given by Dr. Benjamin."

"Dr. Benjamin? You think he left proof. That's why Paxon has been at MIT even though I haven't. It's also why he didn't want me to return last week."

Having to listen to the sadness in her voice was the hardest part of this plan. I wanted to take the earpiece out, but I knew I couldn't. If she and her dad didn't find the evidence on their own tonight, I'd be forced to lead her to it at MIT tomorrow.

"There's more," said her father.

"What?"

"There's evidence suggesting that Irish may have had a hand in Saint's and Benjamin's disappearances."

"What do you need me to do?"

"Two things," said Decker. "First, find the evidence Dr. Benjamin left, and then lead Paxon to the remaining evidence we planted."

"Wait. You don't have Benjamin's evidence already?"

"No. I have enough on Irish without it, but finding it would give us the names of the people he's been working with."

"You don't think Irish knows where it is?" she asked.

"Even if he did, it's unlikely he'd know what he was looking at," said Deck.

"It's in code," she gasped, picking up the second to last bread crumb we'd left for her.

"Do you want to go to MIT tonight?" her father asked.

"That won't be necessary," I heard her answer. "I have what we're looking for at my apartment."

That was it. Everything Decker set up went off like clockwork. Three hours later, I heard Emme's father announce that he'd found the coded evidence we'd planted.

By noon tomorrow, I would be in the custody of federal agents and charged with several counts of conspiracy to spy for China.

"You okay?" Cope asked when he answered my call.

"Scared shitless, if you wanna know the truth." There wasn't anyone I'd admit that to other than Cope. Not even Decker.

"You can trust me."

"That's what I'm counting on."

12

Flynn
Crested Butte, Colorado
September of Previous Year

"Goddamn commie bastard." When my father slammed his fist on the coffee table, I rushed out of the kitchen.

"What?" I asked, drying my hands on a dishtowel.

He pointed at the screen. "Look."

"CIA Officer Arrested for Conspiracy to Spy for China," the news headline read as a man was led away in handcuffs. "Look!" I shouted the same word he had and rushed over to the screen. "That's Buck!"

I watched as my brother moved through the crowd of reporters, escorting the man to the waiting vehicle. Right before getting in, the man who'd been arrested turned and, for a split second, looked straight into the camera. I put my hand on my heart as though I could feel his pain as my eyes looked into his.

My brother's image flashed across the screen a few moments later, and even though he hadn't looked at the camera, something in his expression, too, seemed off.

13

Irish
Richmond, Virginia
January

"What happened with the extraction?" I asked Cope when the guard, really Ink undercover, brought me to the visitation room of the Federal Detention Center in Richmond, Virginia. Before answering, he slowly walked the perimeter of the room.

"What are you doing?"

He put a finger to his lips.

"They got 'em out," he said before sitting down.

"But?"

"Edge took a bullet in his arm. Last I heard, he was in surgery."

"Is Lynx with him?"

Cope nodded. I couldn't explain why that made me feel better, apart from the fact I knew their parents had been killed in a car accident when they were both still kids. From what I'd read, all they had were each other.

"How's Emme?"

Cope sat back in his chair and drummed the table with his fingers. "Upset. By the way, we can talk freely."

"Is that what the walk was about?"

Cope patted his shoulder, which didn't mean jack shit to me. "You know Decker."

"Back to Emme. Is she upset about Edge or me?"

"Worried about Edge. Mad at you. Incredulous that she didn't realize what was going on under her nose."

"That's because it wasn't going on."

"I know that, but I can hardly admit it to her."

Surely, if I had really been a double agent, Dr. Emerson Charles would've been the first to realize it.

"What else?"

"My dad has been asking a lot of questions."

Cope's father was the senior Senator from the State of Louisiana and the sitting chair of the United States Senate Select Committee on Intelligence.

"He's suggesting the agency try harder to make a deal."

"Has he come to you for help making that happen?"

"He brought it up, but I shut him down."

"McTiernan?"

"He asked me to brief him but otherwise hasn't said much."

"My guess is he's trying to determine your involvement."

"I agree."

Cope looked more tired than I remembered ever seeing him.

"If you're worried about me, Ink and Rage won't let anybody touch me."

His eyes met mine. "Was this the right decision, Irish?"

"As long as you and Decker are holding up your end of the bargain."

Cope shook his head, and I saw a glimmer of a smile. "Hard to believe Deck hasn't gotten the whole thing figured out already."

I knew what he meant, but I didn't smile. Given Decker didn't have any leads that I was aware of, this thing was buried deep by people who knew what they were doing and, more importantly, knew how not to get caught.

"Do you think it's China?" he asked.

I'd thought of little else since I arrived here, and no, I didn't think it was. "Maybe involved, but not acting alone."

"I came to the same conclusion, but I'm curious to know why you did."

"Mainly because I can't come up with any reason why a few of the agents killed had nothing to do with Chinese ops, never set foot in mainland China or Hong Kong."

"Who do you think is behind it, then?"

Only one entity made sense to me, and there was no way in hell I'd utter the words out loud.

"What about Dr. Benjamin? Do you think he's involved?" he asked.

I shrugged. "No idea, but I have an equal distrust of Saint."

"I'll be back in a couple of days," Cope said when Ink rapped on the door. "Hammer will be in tomorrow."

"Hammer," I muttered under my breath.

"Decker trusts him."

"And yet he hasn't told him the truth."

"He will when he thinks the time is right."

"In the meantime, he treats me like shit on his shoe."

"Good for your cover."

He might be right, but it was my soul I was more worried about. I thought I was prepared to handle whatever people like the Invincibles' attorney hurled at me. What I hadn't anticipated was the level of vehemence.

While my brain knew I was undercover, playing a role, the impact of others' hatred had a physical effect on my body. I found myself nauseous and in pain frequently. If I were out on bail, something that wasn't a possibility, I would do everything I could to find solace in the arms of a woman, which was even less likely than bail. My body craved the touch of another. I'd take any comfort at all. My pride, though, prevented me from asking for it. Even a simple hug from a man I considered my brother.

"Paxon?"

I looked up at Cope, who had his hand on the doorknob. "Can you do this?"

"Just get it done so I can get the fuck out of here."

* * *

It seemed to take forever for my case to go to trial, and that was with the agency fast-tracking it.

In that time, I'd grown increasingly agitated and angry to the point where there were times I figured Ink and Rage would gladly look the other way if someone did try to kill me.

This morning, Ink, along with two federal marshals, escorted me into a pretrial conference room where Cope was waiting.

"How are you holding up?" he asked.

Instead of answering, I scowled at him.

"Irish?"

"You better be fucking sure you can protect me, Cope."

"You've trusted me this far; don't blow it now by panicking."

"I'm the one locked up in a cell like a goddamn sitting duck."

"Just keep your mouth shut and let me handle it like I always do. If you don't, every risk we've taken in the last seven years will be for nothing."

I understood. I did—intellectually. The depression and anxiety, though, were eating me alive.

Cope drummed the fingers of one hand on the table. "My father ambushed me by inviting Fisk to dinner last night."

The CIA director had been at the top of our list of people we both, along with Decker, believed played a role in the deaths of so many agents, especially when he started snooping around what I was up to prior to my arrest. "And?"

"Smug bastard. It was all I could do not to pull out my gun and shoot the *sonuvabitch*."

I had no doubt I would've felt the same way. And, like Cope, knew that as much as I wanted to kill him, we wouldn't get any answers if he was six feet in the ground.

When I hadn't heard from Cope or Hammer, my acting attorney, in three days, I engaged Ink. Within twenty minutes, he returned with news.

"Hammer says a reporter was driving Cope's car when it was T-boned. I don't know the extent of her injuries, but Cope thinks whoever it was, was targeting him."

"Jesus," I muttered.

"It gets worse."

My eyes opened wide.

"There was a bomb planted in the courtroom. Decker says they're going to bump up security in here."

I didn't say this to Ink, but if we were getting close to nailing these bastards, then they'd stop at nothing to shut us down.

"Who's he bringing in?"

"Easy and Kanga."

"Copy that."

I looked over at Rage, who was undercover as my cellmate. "You wanna transfer out of here, I'll understand."

"Oh, yeah?"

"Yep."

"If that's the case, let's do it together, Irish. I'll ask for a transfer out, and you can come clean to the director.

You know, tell him you've been conducting a side mission for a few years and you're ready to call it quits."

"Fuck you, Rage."

"Yeah, that's what I thought. If you aren't going anywhere, then neither am I."

At three in the morning, an unfamiliar sound woke me. I sat up and saw two men, both guards, rushing toward the cell.

"Rage!" I yelled as I watched Easy, Ink, and Kanga race toward the men, guns firing.

Before I could get out of my bunk and duck for cover, gunfire rained down on the cell. At least four of the bullets hit me before everything went black.

14

Flynn
Crested Butte, Colorado
January

At three this morning, my dad was taken by ambulance from the Roaring Fork Ranch to Gunnison Valley Hospital. Porter was the one who'd found him on the floor in the kitchen. According to the paramedics who came to the house, he'd most likely had a stroke.

"You should stay here," said Cord when I followed him out the front door and over to the truck where Porter and Holt were waiting.

"The hell I will." I stormed past him and climbed into the front passenger seat.

"Flynn—"

"Whatever you're about to say, Port, you can forget. He's my father too."

"He's Buck's father too," Cord said from the back seat.

"I'll call him." There was a chance he was still on the East Coast, where it would be almost daylight.

"Hey, Flynn, I'm in the middle of something, and I'll need to call you back," Buck said, sounding like he'd been awake for some time.

"We're on our way to the hospital. Dad was taken by ambulance." There was silence on the other end of the phone. "Buck, are you there?"

"Shit, Flynn. I'm here. I'm sorry. Been up all night, and I didn't even realize what time it was."

"Buck, you need to come if you want to say goodbye."

"I'll do what I can."

He either ended the call, or it dropped. Either way, it didn't matter.

15

Irish
Richmond, Virginia
February

I tried so damn hard to open my eyes, but I couldn't. The sound of machines beeping their rhythm was muffled in the background just like the voice of the man I'd recognize even half dead—like I knew I was.

"I'm going away for a while, Irish, and as soon as you're able to, you'll be going away too." I could feel his hand wrap around mine. "I'm so damn sorry, Paxon. I promised I'd keep you safe, and I failed." Even as subdued as he sounded, I could hear the emotion in his voice. "I just hope that when this is all over, you can find a way to forgive me."

I tried again to get my damn eyes to open, but they wouldn't budge. Instead, I squeezed his hand with all my might.

"Paxon?"

I squeezed again. It probably didn't feel like much to him, but it took every ounce of strength I possessed. I didn't want to drift out of consciousness again, but my mind couldn't fight against it.

* * *

I opened my eyes and lifted my head.

"Good morning," said Decker, who was sitting in a chair in the corner.

"Where the fuck am I?" I rested my head against the pillow and closed my eyes.

"As I've told you at least ten times now, you're at the King-Alexander Ranch. It's located outside Austin, Texas, and if someone were to attempt to get to you here, their body would be blown to bits. Oh, and like I've said every other time you opened your damned eyes, afterward we could watch the drone footage over and over again if you wanted to."

"What the hell are you talking about?"

"Wouldn't you want to see someone who tried to kill you blown to bits? I sure as hell would."

"Where's Cope?"

I opened my eyes again and looked at Decker. "Undisclosed location, just like you."

"You just told me where I am."

Deck laughed. "You're the only one who knows."

"Other than you."

"Right. I can be forgetful when I need to be."

"How long have I been here?"

"About ten days."

"About?"

Decker laughed again. "Hell, when I'm on the ranch, I don't keep that good a track. One day isn't much different than another. Wake up, do chores, eat, do more chores, eat again, go to bed, sleep, and do it all over again."

"What about the rest of the guys? Ink, Rage, Kanga, and Easy?"

When Decker lowered his head, I knew the news was bad. "Rage got hit, but nothing life-threatening. Ink and Kanga stayed out of the line of fire."

"And Easy?"

"He didn't make it, Irish."

I closed my eyes and turned my head away. Another agent lost. I felt responsible for them all, but none more than Easy. He died protecting me. The man left behind a family, too.

"Irish?"

"Give me a minute, Decker."

"He did his job. He made sure you stayed alive. Although, for quite a while, we weren't sure you would pull through."

"How bad a shape am I in?"

"You've made good progress in your recovery."

I tried to shift my body, but it hurt too damn bad. "You been nursing me yourself?"

"Nah, I've got a team here 'round the clock tending to you. I try to come and give 'em a break every so often so they can take a walk outside, stretch their legs."

"I thought you said no one knows I'm here."

"No one knows Paxon Warrick is here. Your medical team knows you as Charley Weaver."

"You're kidding."

"You must be older than I thought if you know who that is. So far, I haven't seen the slightest indication anyone else does."

I turned my head toward the window, trying to remember the show my grandmother used to watch reruns of.

"*F Troop.*"

"That's what it was," I said, turning back to him. "Would've driven me crazy all day. How'd you know I was trying to think of it?"

"Clairvoyant."

"Wouldn't surprise me."

"Here's your nurse now," said Deck, getting up from the chair. "We'll talk more later." He patted the end of the hospital bed when he walked by.

"Hey, Deck?"

He stuck his head back in the room. "Yeah?"

"Thanks for all this."

He was more jovial than I'd ever seen him, but his expression changed to one I was more familiar with. "We're close, Irish, and all because of your bravery. I know this has been damned hard on you. There will come a day when everyone knows the hero you are. I promise you that."

He turned around and walked away. A few seconds later, a woman dressed in scrubs came in. "You're awake!"

"I am."

"I'm surprised your brother didn't tell me."

"My brother?" I almost told her I didn't have one.

"Well, he said you were half brothers, but he'd never thought of you that way. Anyway, would you like something to eat?"

"What've you got?"

"A cook on standby, ready to make anything that sounds good."

Everything sounded good. I wondered how long it had been since I last ate.

"How about some eggs, bacon, and toast?"

It took another ten days before I was up and around enough that I felt alive. When I finally talked Decker into telling me the extent of my injuries, I wished I hadn't.

"You ready to talk business?" he asked when I came out of the bedroom, showered and dressed in clothes that weren't mine but fit me.

"Sure," I said, pouring myself a cup of coffee which I turned right around and spit out in the sink. "What is this shit?"

"That's cowboy coffee. It'll put hair on your chest."

"I don't need more hair on my chest; I need something drinkable." The coffee the nurses brought me tasted nothing like what I'd just poured into a cup.

Decker motioned with his thumb to one of those pod coffeemakers. "We keep that around for the pussies."

"I've been meaning to ask. Aren't you married?"

"If that segue had anything to do with my wife, know that once you're healed, I'll beat the crap out of you."

I laughed and shook my head. "Nothing of the sort. I was just wondering since I haven't met her."

"That's because she doesn't live here. Neither do I, for that matter. We own the ranch adjacent to King-Alexander. Name's Brandywine. I just come here every day to see how you're doing."

"Wow, Decker, I'm touched."

"Yeah, whatever. You wanna work or lie on your ass in that bed every day?"

"What've you got?"

Two hours later, my head was pounding and I wanted nothing more than to take a nap. But I couldn't. I still had pages of information to sort through, but the bottom line was, Decker had enough on Ed Fisk to take him down along with several of the handlers and operatives who made up a vast network of double agents. China was behind most of it, but not all. Just like Cope and I thought.

"This is the second dirty director in a row," I muttered, reading over the evidence Decker had compiled on Fisk.

"Not exactly a coincidence, Irish."

"Right. I just hope the next guy has nothing to do with Flatly, Fisk, Montgomery—anyone associated with that bunch."

"Let's just say I am only one of a few who intend to have some say in who they give the job to next."

"Glad to hear it."

Decker stood and stretched. "While I'd like to say I'm the one who found most of this, I have to give credit where it's due. Senator Copeland put the full force of the intelligence committee behind this one. McTiernan too."

"What happens next?"

"Carefully choreographed arrests around the world."

"When?"

"Two weeks from today."

I got up and walked through the front door and out onto the stone patio that went all the way around the house. I couldn't wrap my head around the fact that this was it. Seven years of work would culminate in bringing down the Director of the CIA, plus a world-wide network of double agents.

So why didn't it feel like it would soon be over? When would the fear of knowing that every day could bring the death of more agents end? When would the night come that I could fall asleep without feeling I had no right to? Or wake in the morning without dread in the pit of my stomach?

"Irish?"

When Decker came outside, I was sitting in a chair, bent at the waist, head in my hands, crying like a baby. "Leave it alone, Deck."

"You got it. I'll see you tomorrow."

I didn't look, but I heard his truck start up and drive away.

**

It happened the last day of February—the twenty-eighth since it wasn't leap year. Fisk was the first to be taken down but only by a few seconds. Law enforcement agencies around the world assisted, but it was teams of US Marshals that carried out the arrests. Only men and women vetted by Decker Ashford, Senator Henry Clay Copeland, and Kellen McTiernan were tasked with carrying out orders that would shake the intelligence world to its core.

Cope contacted me at dawn—via a video call. It was the first time I heard his voice since the day in the hospital when I didn't have the strength to respond. The last time I saw him was at the federal courthouse.

Today, my voice was strangled with emotion and I had to turn my head to hide my tears.

"This is it, Irish. You did it."

I shook my head and looked back at my phone's screen. "We did it."

"It never would've happened without you, Paxon."

"How's Ali?" I asked, needing to deflect attention I wasn't prepared to handle.

"I haven't seen her yet."

"When will you?"

"Later this morning."

"I'm happy for you, Cope. I hope it works out between the two of you."

"I've got something to ask you."

"Shoot."

"Never mind. There's something I need to ask her first."

* * *

One month later, Cope asked Ali—the reporter who had been T-boned in his car and who he fell in love with while I was in jail—to marry him. The same night, he asked me to be his best man. I was glad for him, truly, but I couldn't shake the feeling of dread in the pit of my stomach. I wondered if it would ever go away. I wouldn't tell him that, though. I wouldn't spoil his happiness.

"Hey, you," said Ali, coming out to the backyard of Cope's parents' house.

"Congratulations," I said, hugging her.

"Best wishes."

"Huh?"

"You congratulate the man and offer best wishes to the woman."

"Yeah? I don't know much about shit like that."

Ali pulled me over to the garden bench. "Someday, you will. I hope it's soon, Irish. You deserve happiness, maybe more than anyone I know."

Did I? On the day of the arrests, I asked Decker if he'd kept count of the agents killed. He shook his head, but I didn't believe him. I would trust, though, it was a number I didn't want to know.

16

Irish
Washington, DC
May

"This is a wedding, not a damn job interview," I said to Money McTiernan, who had me cornered at the bar for the last fifteen minutes.

"It isn't an interview, Irish. I'm asking you to take the same job you had before."

I knew the answer to my next question, but I'd ask anyway. "Is Cope?"

Money motioned to the bartender with two fingers. I really didn't need another drink, but what the fuck, it wasn't every day your best friend, the man you went to hell and back with, got married.

"I'm going to wait until after he and Ali return from their honeymoon to ask."

"You're trying to get her to come back too, aren't you?"

While Ali had been undercover as a reporter covering my trial, her real job was as an internal affairs agent for the CIA. It was the only division that operated independently, and for good reason. Ali had originally been brought in by Money to ascertain whether Cope was also a double agent who had betrayed his country like many believed I was.

A few still hadn't received the memo that I'd been undercover too, and couldn't stop themselves from looking at me like the traitor I wasn't.

I looked across the yard at one in particular. TJ Hunter was her name, and she was actually a reporter. She and Cope had been friends for a long time. I also got the feeling she wanted more, but that was when neither of us had the brain space to think about relationships. Although, when Cope met Ali, he found some quickly.

My gaze met Stella's—a nickname Cope had given her, and everyone used—and I raised my glass. As I anticipated, she didn't do the same. Instead, she turned away.

"It'll take time," said Money, watching the exchange.

"You know what? I really don't give a shit."

I walked away, planning to find a quiet place inside the house where I didn't have to see or talk to anyone. Before I reached the door, Decker intercepted me.

"Tell me you're not thinking of going back to the agency."

I laughed. "Why? You got a job offer for me?"

"More than that, Irish, and you know it. We want you to come on board as a partner."

"I don't know. I'm not sure I can work for a company that calls themselves the Invincibles."

"Fucking Rile," Decker mumbled. "I never should've gone along with it."

Everyone knew it had been Rile who came up with the name. And coming from him, it hadn't been a surprise. The guy was an arrogant asshole, as far as I was concerned, and I couldn't stand him. Then again, there weren't many people I could stand.

Cope, sometimes. Decker, sometimes. Ali, sometimes. It was a short list.

"I need some time, Deck."

"I know you do, and I'll quit pestering you. What I won't do is let you go back to the agency."

"What about another firm?"

"If you're about to say K19, I'll…"

K19 Security Solutions was the Invincibles' equal and rival when it came to private intelligence and covert ops firms. A guy named Doc Butler headed it up with some partners. Doc hadn't made me an offer, but if he did, it would be a damned hard decision to make if it weren't for the fact that I owed Decker my life. "You'll what?" I asked.

"Hell, I don't know. I'd say I'd never forgive you, but that makes me sound like a pussy."

I laughed and squeezed his shoulder. "Decker, you should know without asking that if I were to go private, I'd have to sign up with the Invincibles."

"Why do I think you're blowing smoke up my ass?"

I shook my head and walked away.

Less than a week later, I got a call from Decker. When I saw it was him, everything inside me screamed not to answer. Somehow, I knew this wasn't about the job offer. Somehow, I knew my instincts were right—it wasn't over. Not even close. We may have taken down Fisk and a few of his henchmen, but we hadn't gotten everyone.

"Yeah?"

"Irish. We need to meet."

"When and where?"

"You don't sound surprised."

"My gut's been on high alert."

"I didn't want to admit it, but mine has too. Rock is on his way to get you now."

"Get me?"

"You're going back into protective custody."

"King-Alexander?"

"Nah, but you are going to a ranch. This one is in Colorado."

"Where are you?"

"In DC. Rock will bring you to the airfield. I'll brief you then."

Ritter "Rock" Johnson had worked for the Invincibles since leaving the CIA before my official "departure." While he and I had never shared a mission, I knew he was one of the best there was in terms of asset protection.

I shook my head. That's what I'd become—an asset.

17

Flynn
Crested Butte, Colorado
May

Four years ago, the doctors told my father he wouldn't live six more months. He showed them and us, his kids.

Like he had in life, he controlled us from the grave. Not all of us, just his oldest son, Buck.

When Buck left the ranch to go to college, our father told him that if he did, he'd never own a piece of the property that had been in our family for over one hundred years. Today, after my father's attorney read his will, there wasn't a single one of us who believed we'd inherit any of it.

My father, the cantankerous *sonuvabitch* that he was, issued an ultimatum through his last will and testament. If Buck didn't spend an entire year living full-time on the Roaring Fork Ranch, which was defined as not being away from the ranch for longer than forty-eight consecutive hours, then everything—the ranch and all our family's assets—would be given to charity.

That wasn't all. In the same period of time, Buck was expected to bring the ranch that had been operating in the red since our dad got sick, into the black. *In one year.*

Every ounce of sadness I felt when he died turned into anger. How could he do this to Buck?

I almost wished we had known he was pulling this before the visitation and funeral because there was no way in hell I would've asked Buck to attend had I known.

My heart ached for my oldest brother, especially when he got up and walked out before the attorney was finished.

Within moments, the rest of us got up, one by one, and left too.

"Are you okay?" Holt asked Buck when he came outside with Cord a few minutes after I had.

"We'll talk when we get back to the ranch."

"That was fucked up," said Porter, storming past the rest of us.

"Sorry," I said to him, not knowing what else to say. He put his arm around my shoulders.

"We'll talk once we're home."

I looked into his eyes. "You said 'home.'"

"Don't make too much of that."

I couldn't stand it. Since we got home, Buck hadn't come out of his room, and Porter was angrier than I'd ever seen him. Something told me it wasn't at our dad, either, which wasn't fair.

"Buck?" I said, knocking on his door.

"I'll be out in a minute, Flynn."

"Can I come in?"

He opened the door.

"I'm sure this is hard for you to accept."

He shook his head. "That is an understatement, sis."

"I know you and Pop never got along much, but I believe in my heart, he did what he thought was best for the ranch and best for our family."

"I'm not your savior. Not any of yours. If things are as bad as Porter says and the four of you want the ranch, you're going to have to work your asses off. I didn't bring any magic bullets with me."

"It won't matter how hard we work if you leave, Buck."

"Are you leavin'?" asked Cord, who was standing in the doorway, listening to us like Holt and Porter were.

"Hell, no, I'm not leaving."

I threw my arms around Buck's neck. "Thank you," I whispered right before he got up and stormed out, motioning for Porter to follow.

"I can't believe he'd do this," said Holt a little while later, coming inside from the barn.

"Who and what?"

Cord walked in behind him. "Buck is leaving."

"What? No! He just said he wasn't."

"There's an emergency. A murder."

"I can't believe it," I said under my breath, looking out the window at where Buck was pacing and on his cell phone.

When Porter walked in, our eyes met. "What are we going to do, Port?" I asked.

"Start packing."

"He said he'd be back within the forty-eight hours," said Cord.

"And you're a fool enough to believe him?"

I looked out the window at Buck. He was off the phone and headed our way. "I believe him."

"I believe him too," said Holt.

"Hell, I gotta too, then," muttered Cord.

"Well, I don't gotta," snapped Porter, going into his room and slamming the door.

"What choice do we have?" I said, not really asking or expecting an answer.

"None," said Holt.

"Absolutely none," added Cord.

18

The plane we flew on was a private one, owned by the Invincibles. When I boarded, I saw Buck Wheaton already seated beside TJ "Stella" Hunter, the reporter who had covered my trial and whom I'd seen with Buck at Cope and Ali's wedding.

Decker motioned Rock and me to the rear of the plane. "Have a seat. After takeoff, I'll brief you on what's gone down."

"Roger that," I muttered, thankful that Rock didn't sit right next to me. The idea that he or anyone else would be on my detail was something I'd have to get used to. When I was recovering at the King-Alexander Ranch, the elaborate security system Decker had set up served as my detail.

When I heard the chimes indicating we could get up and walk around, I followed Deck into a stateroom. Rock joined us and closed the door behind him.

"You're probably wondering what Stella is doing on board," Decker began.

"I wonder a lot of things."

He smirked. "As you're aware, Stella and Ali were writing a book about the mission you and Cope undertook and that I joined in on."

Of course I was aware, and I was against it, not that anyone had asked me, even though it was my fucking story.

"Does the name Barb Hunter mean anything to you?" asked Decker.

"Stella's aunt."

"That's right. Ten years ago, she was considered to be one of the best investigative journalists in the business."

"Then what happened?" I asked.

"She wrote a piece accusing members of Interpol of accepting bribes in exchange for a massive cover-up of what she reported as being called Operation Argead."

"Right. I remember now. There was something about her having an affair with Interpol's president and writing the story after he dumped her."

"That man was Nicholas Kerr. A bit of an enigma. Anyway, the day after Cope and Ali's wedding, Stella paid her aunt a visit. While Barb had asked Stella to abandon the book before, this time, she took it a step further. They argued, and Barb warned Stella that if she didn't walk away, they might both end up paying with their lives.

"Three days later, Stella paid Barb another visit and found her and her housekeeper dead. Both had been shot at point-blank range."

"You believe Barb's story from ten years ago relates to Fisk somehow?"

"I do, and that's why you're here, Irish. First, if I'm right—and I almost always am—you remain in danger. Second, if it does, it means our mission isn't over."

Buck joined us an hour later, and we talked about how things would proceed once we arrived at his family's ranch. Most of it had little to do with me other than it would be the place where I'd be living for the foreseeable future.

"This is my plan," said Decker. "I've got a crew headed to the ranch now. They should already be there by the time we land. I'll get them started on setup of the new security system, and head to California to meet with Burns. Rock can take over until I return."

Burns Butler had been Decker's mentor when he was barely out of high school. While the man was renowned in the intelligence world as a technological genius—like Decker was—he was also considered the best in the business when it came to making everything to do with an op, or even an entire mission, disappear in a way that made it seem like it had never happened. In other words, burning it.

Decker turned to me. "Your job is to find out everything you can about Kerr and his tenure at Interpol."

"Roger that," I said as Deck and Buck left the stateroom.

"How're you doin', Irish?" asked Rock.

"You know how you feel when you're having a nightmare and you wake up, but then you go back to sleep and the nightmare starts up again? That's how I'm doing."

"I hear ya. I'm sorry, Irish. We all thought it was over."

Part II

19

Irish

Buck led Rock, Stella, and me into the ranch's main house. "Hello?" he called out.

"Hey, Buck," I heard a female's voice answer and saw a woman walk up to hug him.

"Where is everybody?" he asked.

"Out surveying." The woman turned and looked directly at me. "Who are you?"

"Paxon Warrick," I said, stepping forward and extending my hand. When she took it, a feeling I couldn't explain, other than to say I never wanted her to let go, washed over me.

"Flynn Wheaton," she said. Her cheeks flushed, and I gripped her hand tighter.

"Great name," I said.

"Yours too."

When Buck tapped her on the shoulder, I dropped her hand. "Hey, sis, I'd like you to meet my friend Stella. Stella, this is Flynn."

I watched as they shook hands; I couldn't take my eyes off Buck's sister. Buck's sister. I knew from the brief that he didn't have more than one, which meant Flynn was twenty-one years old. What I'd give to take ten years off my age and be five years older than her rather than fifteen.

"And this is Decker Ashford and Rock Johnson," I heard Buck say.

"It's nice to meet you both." Flynn was polite, shaking the hands of both men while looking over her shoulder at me more than once. How did I know? Because I hadn't taken my eyes off her.

"Stella and Irish…err…Paxon are going to be spending some time here, on the ranch."

When Buck walked in the direction of the hallway, I wished Stella would go with him so I could talk to Flynn alone.

"We'll go get settled," Buck said to Stella before turning to me. "You too, Irish."

"I should head out now too, but I'm sure I'll see you later," said Flynn, taking a step closer to me.

"I'd like that." I followed her to the front door and watched her walk away.

"Ready?" I heard Buck say. When I turned around, I saw he was carrying a travel bag.

"Where are you going?" I asked.

"I'll be staying in one of the cabins."

"Which one?"

"I'm not sure it matters, but if you're asking if I'm staying with you, the answer is no."

"Hey, Irish, you do know I'm writing a book about the Fisk mission," Stella said as we walked out the front door. "I was hoping that since we're both here for the foreseeable future, you could tell me more about it."

"You have other sources." I didn't care if I came off as rude.

First of all, the book was the reason we were all here. Did she think I wasn't aware of that fact? Second, the woman didn't know the first thing about me, but she'd hated me on sight and had never attempted to hide it. Even now, knowing I didn't do any of the things she thought I had, she hadn't apologized for the way she'd treated me.

We got into a Ford truck, old enough that it still had a bench seat, giving me no choice but to sit next to her. She inched closer to Buck, which didn't bother me in the slightest.

"You're in that one down there," Buck said after pulling up to three cabins in close proximity to one another. I grabbed my bag from the bed of the pickup and walked down to the cabin. Only when I got to the front door did it dawn on me that it might be locked. I reached out and the handle turned. I pulled my gun from its holster and eased my way inside, only to find Ink sitting on the sofa. When he saw my gun, he laughed.

"You're lucky I didn't shoot."

"Right," he said, shaking his head as if he either thought I was a lousy shot or he was bulletproof.

I dropped my bag on the floor and was about to see if there was anything in the fridge when my cell rang. Ink got up and went outside without my needing to ask.

"Cope, aren't you supposed to be on your honeymoon?"

"Hey, Irish. I heard Stella's aunt was murdered. Deck thinks this might be somehow tied to Fisk."

"Apparently, the aunt warned her that if she didn't drop writing the book, it would put both of their lives in danger."

"What I have to tell you makes me think Barb may have been right. The federal prosecutor offered Fisk a deal, which he refused to take."

"Fuck." Both Cope and I believed Fisk would turn state's evidence as soon as it was offered. The only reason he wouldn't, would be if he knew someone had the means to silence him if he did.

"Fisk is more afraid of what will happen if he makes a deal than he is of going to prison," said Cope.

"My thoughts exactly. What about some of the other people arrested?"

"The prosecutor is only interested in what Fisk has to say. Hey, is Buck around?"

"He's next door."

"Do you want to brief him on this, or do you want me to?"

"I'll let you. We just got here, and I need to take care of a few things."

When the call ended, I walked back to the fridge, relieved to see it was stocked with food along with a few beers. I pulled one out, twisted the cap, and took a long swig. I sat down on the sofa and looked around.

When Buck said we'd be staying in cabins, I hadn't known what to expect, but it sure as hell wasn't this.

The room I was in looked straight out of a magazine or a movie set. The sofa I sat on was oversized and so damned comfortable, I thought about stretching out and taking a nap.

I did succumb to putting my feet up, but I doubted I could sleep. My brain raced with the things Decker had told Buck, Rock, and me on the flight here.

My phone vibrating jarred me out of my stupor. I picked it up and read the text from Decker.

We're meeting next door, it said.

I could only guess that meant the cabin Stella was staying in.

When I knocked, it appeared Buck wasn't expecting me. Before I could explain, Decker walked up behind me. Buck's pretty sister followed, pushing past both of us.

"Hey, everybody," she said.

"What are you doing here, Flynn?" Buck asked.

"Holt asked if anyone would mind if Ben Rice and a couple guys from his band came over tonight."

"It would be better if Holt went there instead."

"But—"

"We're in the middle of something, Flynn," Buck said to her.

I pulled out my laptop when Decker did, sat at the table, and covered my mouth to hide my grin when she turned on her heel and stomped toward the door.

"I'll go with you, Flynn," I heard Stella say.

"You need to stay here," Buck told her.

"I'm just going back to the house, Buck," said Flynn. I was half tempted to get up from my chair and tell her I'd go with her as well. There was something that drew me to her. Crazy as it sounded, even to me, it was as though her soul spoke to mine, and it was the kindest I'd ever known.

"I said Stella needs to stay here."

"Buck, I—"

Before Stella could finish whatever she was going to say, Buck took her hand and pulled her into the bedroom.

"I'll walk you out," I said to Flynn, happy for the chance to be alone with her, even for a couple of minutes.

"I guess whatever you're doing is pretty important," she said, kicking a rock off the cabin's front porch.

"It is."

She looked out at the horizon and then at me. "Um, if you need anything, let me know and I'll take care of it."

"What kinds of anything?"

Her cheeks turned pink, and she grinned.

How long had it been since I flirted? Years, it seemed, other than with Emme—who I'd heard was now married to Lynx.

Thinking about it reminded me I had no business flirting now. If Decker's suspicions were correct, and I had no doubt they were, our mission was still underway.

"I'll let you get back to it," Flynn said, turning to leave.

"Wait. What kinds of things?"

"You know, food, extra towels, other stuff for the cabin…"

"If I do need those things, how do I get in touch with you?"

Her cheeks were pink again, and she lowered her gaze. "I guess I should give you my number."

"Do you give your number to all the guests?"

"You're the first one."

"The first one you've given your number to?"

"The first guest."

"Go ahead," I said, typing it into my phone as she rattled off the numbers.

"Okay, well, bye."

"I'll see you later, Flynn."

She walked away, waving behind her, and I went inside.

"Are they still in there?" I asked Decker.

"Mm-hmm," he grumbled.

The door opened seconds later, and Buck came out.

"Where's Stella?" Decker asked.

"She'll be out in a minute."

"We're gonna need her."

"If I go back in there—"

Deck held up his hand. "That was the last thing I was suggesting. Believe me."

Stella came out and sat in the chair Buck pulled out for her.

"I spoke with Burns," Deck began. "He said he's heard rumors about Operation Argead but never had a reason to look into it. Which means he didn't burn it. He has theories about who did, though, and has promised to see what he can find out. For now, there's no reason for me to go to California."

"Copy that," both Buck and I said.

"There's more."

"What?" Buck asked.

"Settle down, young Buck. I'm getting to it."

"You do know that you're only a couple of years older than I am, right?"

"In age maybe, but infinitely older in wisdom."

Instead of sitting here, listening to this bullshit, I wished I could get up, go outside, call Flynn, and give her a list of things I needed from her, none of which included food, towels, or anything else for the cabin.

"Burns thinks it would be best if we kept this thing as far away from the Invincibles as possible. Mainly to keep the heat off Irish and Stella. Cope and Ali too." Decker looked over at me.

"What did he suggest?" I asked.

"To pull K19 in."

Both Buck and I raised a brow. An Invincibles partner was suggesting bringing in a rival company?

"Yeah, I don't like it either, but hear me out."

"What's the plan?" I asked.

"This is the part I like. Cope will contact Doc and get him to contract out a couple of undercover gigs."

"Where?"

"Inside Interpol, for one."

"Who are you thinking?"

"Casper."

The choice surprised me. Calla "Casper" Rey did far more work with the Invincibles than with any other private firm. I knew because her husband, Beau, was one of the agents whose death had gone unexplained, forcing Casper to resign from the agency when she couldn't get any answers about how he'd died. I knew Casper well and admired her.

"Who else?" asked Buck.

"I'll leave that to Doc."

"Why did you say you liked the part of the plan where Cope contacts Doc?" Stella asked.

"I'll answer that," said Buck. "Because Doc will think it means he's got a shot at recruiting Cope to join up with them."

"Does he?" she asked.

"Hell no," muttered Decker.

"Cope won't sign with the Invincibles either." When I spoke, all eyes turned to me.

"We'll see," said Deck.

"What'll Casper's assignment be?" Buck asked.

"To get inside Interpol's executive committee. If we can get her in place quickly enough, she can be set up in time for the end-of-quarter meetings."

Interpol served as a clearinghouse for international crime intel, rather than an actual law enforcement agency. The organization only had as much power as its executive committee, and of the three positions—president, vice president, and secretary-general—only the latter was a full-time, paid position.

The other two offices were advisory in nature and held by individuals who still worked for their respective countries' intelligence agencies. The committee only met officially at the end of each quarter. Everyone in intelligence believed they met far more often than that in an unofficial capacity.

"Does Fisk have any connection to Interpol?" Buck asked.

"Negative," Deck answered.

"What about Kerr?" asked Stella. "Does he have any connection to the current executive committee?"

"Irish?" prompted Deck.

As he instructed on the plane, I'd spent the rest of the flight learning as much as I could about the man Stella just asked about, along with his connections.

"Both Daniel Byrne, the current president, and Boris Antonov, his vice, served as delegates under Kerr. I haven't been able to find a connection to Kim Ha-joon, the secretary-general, yet. However, he's tight with Byrne and Antonov."

"What about a connection between Kerr and Fisk?"

I wasn't prepared to answer questions from a reporter, so I didn't. "Need-to-know."

Decker cleared his throat. "Irish, answer Stella's question."

There were times Decker's high-handedness pissed me the fuck off. "They worked together at CFR."

"CFR?" Buck asked.

Stella pushed back her chair, stood, and walked over to the window. "The Council on Foreign Relations."

"Officially, it's a foreign policy think tank. Unofficially, a place for its 'members' to meet without having to announce it as such," I explained to Buck.

"Which office?" Stella asked.

"Fisk was in DC. Kerr was in New York."

"Barb too?" Buck asked.

"New York office," she responded.

There it was. The line had been drawn between Stella's aunt, Kerr, and Fisk. That hadn't taken long.

"What happened to him?" Buck asked.

"Kerr? He stayed on at MI5, but not as director general, the position he'd held for years," I told him.

"What did he do instead?"

"Consultant."

"Where did Kerr go after that?" Stella asked.

"Retired." Something occurred to me, and my eyes met hers.

"What?" she asked.

"He divorced his wife at the same time he left Interpol. He's been married to Sally Hennessey for nine years."

"Jesus fucking Christ." Stella stalked out of the cabin door.

"Who's that?" Buck asked, standing to follow her.

"At the time, she was the executive editor at AP."

"Barb's editor?" Deck asked.

"Affirmative."

A few minutes later, Stella came back in. Buck wasn't with her.

"Hey, Deck, can I have a minute with Irish?" she asked.

Jesus, first Decker, now her? It was one thing to take his shit. I had no intention of taking hers.

"I was just getting ready to head out anyway." He put his laptop in his bag and slung it over his shoulder.

"Are you leaving the ranch?"

"As soon as I make sure Rock has the install of the security system under control, I'm headed to Texas."

After Decker left, Stella sat down at the table. "Look, Paxon, I owe you an apology, and it's long past due."

I nodded but didn't say anything.

"I know you're a good man, and you deserve a lot better than has been doled out to you, including by me. But now, I'm part of the investigation. The same people you're after either killed my aunt or arranged for someone else to do it. I'm going to take them down, Irish, if it's the last thing I do."

"Copy that."

"Can we figure out a way to work together on this?"

"I promised Decker I would." I stood to leave.

"Where are you going?"

I wanted to tell her I didn't answer to her. Instead, I told her I work better alone.

"But—"

"Whatever I find, I'll share."

"Everything good?" Buck asked when I went outside.

"I told Decker I'd work with Stella if that's what you're referring to."

"I consider that good."

"Whatever." I returned to my cabin. Once there, I tried to figure out an excuse to contact Flynn, but I couldn't come up with anything. Instead, I decided to continue looking into Nicholas Kerr.

As I'd told Stella earlier, once he left Interpol, he went back to work for SIS, but only in an advisory position. There wasn't a lot about what he'd been up to in the last ten years, which I found suspicious. How did someone go from being that big of a player, to a man of little influence in such a short amount of time? The answer was, he hadn't. He'd just gotten quieter about it.

On a whim, I decided to look up his travel records and hit pay dirt. I grabbed my computer and rushed next door.

When I got there, I could see Buck and Stella inside.

"What?" Buck snapped when he opened the door.

"Where did Stella go?"

"To get dressed, asshole."

"What the hell?"

"You could see us. It didn't occur to you to take a hike and come back later?"

"Sorry to interrupt your little interlude, but while you're playing kissy-face with the reporter, there are agents out there in the world getting killed."

Stella came out of the bedroom. "Irish, was there something you wanted to talk to me about?"

"I was able to obtain travel records for Kerr."

"And?"

"He flew from England to New York City two days before your aunt's death. According to the manifest, he was on the plane. Once Decker is at King-Alexander, he'll be able to delve into facial recognition in order to determine Kerr's whereabouts."

"Two questions."

"Go ahead."

"Can you please remind me what King-Alexander is again?"

"A large ranch in Texas that has been Decker's home since he was a teenager. It's owned by Z Alexander and his two adult children. Actually, I misspoke. Since Decker and Mila married, they've resided on her ranch, which is adjacent to King-Alexander. That reminds me, Decker heard back from Z about Kerr. He said there was nothing remarkable about him retiring from full-time duty with MI5 and becoming a consultant. It happens all the time. What was your other question?"

"Any idea of Hennessey's whereabouts?"

"She's believed to still be in London. Again, once Decker is available, he'll track her."

"Was there anything else?"

"I thought you'd want to know about Kerr's arrival in the States right away."

"Thank you very much for that information."

"Thanks, Irish," said Buck.

I was almost to my cabin when a truck drove up. Flynn was behind the wheel.

"Hey, there," I said, walking over to open her door. "Are you making a delivery?"

She cocked her head.

"Next door?"

"Um, no. Buck knows where to get whatever he needs."

"I see."

"What? I mean, what do you see?"

I took a step closer to her. "Why did you stop by, Flynn?"

"Oh! The concert! My brother Holt, you met him, right?"

"I don't think I have."

"You will. Anyway, he's in a band. Kind of a famous band, and they're playing a set at one of the other ranches. I came by to ask Buck if you all wanted to go."

"Does that include me?"

She smiled. "Of course it does."

"I'll answer for myself, then. Yes, I'd like to go."

"Buck might not think it's a good idea." When Flynn bit her bottom lip, I was tempted to reach out and touch her chin.

"Do you think it's his decision?"

"You know...the whole safety thing."

"You're aware of that?"

"Not the details, but yeah."

I pointed to where Ink was standing. "See that guy?"

"Yes."

"He's here to protect both Stella and me. There are more guys like him hanging around. If I want to go somewhere, then one or more of them will go with me. Okay?"

"Okay. So, you really want to go?"

"More than anything." I loved the way she smiled at my words. I wanted to see more of it. "Go ask your brother if he and Stella want to go too."

"Is he over there?"

"Yep. I just got done talking to him."

20

Flynn

I had never wanted to be invisible more than I did right now. I knew Paxon was watching me walk away and was taking in the view of how fat my ass looked in my Wrangler jeans and how my stringy hair hung down my back with no style whatsoever. I wasn't one of those girls who stared into a mirror, wishing I was skinnier or prettier. I didn't have time. Except right now, I wished I was.

Without thinking, I jimmied the door handle and walked into the cabin. "Hey, Buck," I said when he came out of the bedroom.

"What are you doing here, Flynn?"

"Sorry if I'm intruding."

"Knock next time."

I felt my cheeks flush and wanted to turn around and walk out, but I wanted Paxon to be able to go tonight more.

"Instead of CB Rice coming here, Holt is inviting everyone to the Flying R Ranch. They're going to perform a full set."

"What are you asking?"

"If we could all go."

"Not a good idea."

"Come on, Buck. It'll be fun."

"I don't know, Flynn. I'm not sure I want to risk leaving the ranch."

"Have you ever been on the Flying R? With as famous as Ben Rice is, I'd be willing to bet their security system is as elaborate as the one being installed here."

"I doubt it, but I hadn't thought about the fact that Ben would need something substantial."

"It'll mean so much to Holt."

"When did he become a member of Ben's band?"

"A couple of years ago. Until he knew whether they'd invite him to go on tour, he kept it quiet."

"Did I hear something about going to see a band?" asked Stella, also coming out of the bedroom.

"I'm trying to talk my overprotective brother into coming along and bringing you and Paxon with him."

"What if we ask some of the guys working on the security system to go along?" Stella asked.

My brother stroked his beard. "That could work."

"Please," I begged, clasping my hands together.

"Let me talk to Rock first, and I'll let you know."

When I walked out of the cabin, Paxon was still out on the porch of his. "Well?"

"He's talking it over with Rock."

Paxon nodded.

"The thing is, the guy who owns the ranch is a mega rock star. He probably has more security at his place than we do here."

He motioned me to go over to him, and we both sat down on the porch swing.

"Your brother also has to think about the other people who might be at this place. He doesn't have time to secure a guest list and vet it."

"I didn't think about that," I said, feeling like an idiot.

"You wouldn't have any reason to. I hope once we're gone, you have no reason to again. You should never have to live your life in fear."

"There are other things to fear in life besides someone wanting to kill me," I said, wishing I had thought it rather than said it out loud.

Paxon leaned over so we were almost close enough to touch.

"Like what, Flynn?"

I looked out over the ranch. "Nothing," I mumbled. "I just meant in general."

Paxon reached for my hand and ran the pad of his thumb over the back of it. "What things are there to fear in your life, Flynn?"

I shook my head, and my eyes filled with tears.

"You don't know me that well, but you can talk to me."

Maybe I could, if I could speak. I knew that if I did, I'd probably cry harder.

"I don't know how much you've been told about who I am or why I'm here, but last year, I was undercover on an assignment that required me to make people believe I was a spy for another country."

I turned my head to look at him. "I saw your arrest on television."

"That was part of the assignment too. Anyway, the way people treated me then was something I never want to experience again in my life. When I was in the thick of it, I dreaded the look in people's eyes when they saw me, or even just their expressions. They had so much hatred for me, and there was nothing I could do or say to defend myself."

"That must've been awful."

"It was harder than I thought it would be. Much harder, in fact."

"They're nicer now, though, right?"

"For the most part, although there are still people who see me as a traitor."

"But you're not."

"Can't turn those feelings off with a switch, though."

"That makes sense."

Paxon studied me, but I wasn't ready to tell him what I lived in fear of. It was too humiliating to say I feared people calling me "heifer" and him or anyone else hearing it. Maybe he wouldn't be able to flip a switch on seeing me that way himself.

I stood and put my hands in my pockets. "I have to get back to work. I hope my brother figures out a way that you and Stella can go to the Flying R with us tonight."

"I hope so too, Flynn."

I loved the way he looked at me, and at the same time, I hated it. I so wanted to believe he was attracted to me, but I was sure he was no different than any other man who saw me as fat and dumpy.

21

Irish

Flynn's pain sat so close to the surface that it seeped from her pores in the same way her tears did from her eyes.

I wished she'd talk to me, confide in me, let me comfort and reassure her, but why would she? We'd only met earlier today. If I thought about it from that perspective, what made me think I had any right to ask?

I was still on the porch when Buck stalked out of the cabin next door. He walked over to his pickup without a word. When he threw stones driving away, I laughed.

Evidently, the honeymoon was over with Stella. It wasn't surprising that it hadn't lasted long. She was a fucking bitch as far as I was concerned.

Not long after, Rock drove up.

"Trouble in paradise?" I shouted.

"Something like that."

"Heard there was a band playing at one of the neighboring ranches tonight."

"Right. We'll head out at about five thirty."

The happiness I felt over hearing we were going, stunned me. Maybe it was just having a semblance of normalcy, even with bodyguards, that buoyed my spirits.

I met Stella and Rock outside when it was time to leave, somewhat surprised Buck wasn't with them. I offered to sit in the back, like I would've anyway, pleased when Rock said we had one more to pick up, hoping it would be Flynn.

When she got in the truck, beside me, she sighed and fidgeted enough that it led me to believe she was uncomfortable. She hadn't been that way with me before, so I wondered what was causing it.

When she twirled her hair with her finger, I reached out and touched her hand.

"You look very pretty."

Instead of smiling or even blushing, Flynn looked perplexed.

"What?" I asked.

"You don't have to say that," she mumbled.

I moved my hand to her chin and turned her head so I could look into her eyes. "Flynn, you look very pretty."

"Thank you," she said, trying to turn away, but I wasn't ready to release her gaze. Her eyes darted toward the front seat, making me realize this wasn't the time or place to have this conversation. Flynn was already uncomfortable enough.

When we arrived at the other ranch, I realized we'd been traveling as a caravan. "Wait there," I said to Flynn, jumping out and coming around to open her door. She smiled and took my hand when I offered it.

The band was already playing when we walked into the barn. I was surprised to see so many people dancing.

"What first?" I asked. "Drink or a dance?"

"Do you really want to dance?"

I pointed in the direction of the couples. "I don't know how to do fancy stuff like that, but I would like to dance with you."

We were headed in that direction when another man approached us.

"Flynn?" he said, looking her up and down.

Her eyes scrunched, and she shook her head as though she didn't want him to say anything else.

"Where did you get that dress—"

"Porter, have you met Paxon Warrick? He's a guest at the Roaring Fork. Paxon, this is my brother Porter."

"Nice to meet you," I said, holding my hand out.

"Nice to meet you too." Porter looked at his sister and then at me.

"We were headed out to the dance floor, if you'll excuse us."

I put my hand on the small of Flynn's back, and she flinched. When we were far enough away from her brother, I asked her about it. "If you'd rather not dance, it's okay."

"Would you rather not?"

I looked into her eyes and smiled. "I asked you to, which means I'd very much like to."

Flynn was stiff as a board in my arms, but that wouldn't stop me from holding her. I kept my grip loose and, as she relaxed, gradually pulled her closer to me. We didn't do much more than step from side to side, even when the song went from slow to fast.

"Did you want to get a drink?" she asked when we were on our third song.

"Not as much as I want to keep dancing."

"Oh. Uh. Okay."

I chuckled, took her hand in mine, and led her over to the bar.

We were getting close when another man—based on how much he resembled the first one, I guessed he was another brother—approached us. "Flynn?"

"Yes, it's me. God, do you really have to make such a big deal out of how I'm dressed? Cord, this is Paxon Warrick. Paxon, this is my brother Cord." She pointed toward the stage. "The guy with the red shirt is my brother Holt. I'm sure if the band takes a break, he'll be equally shocked by my attire as Cord and Porter were. Oh, and Buck will be too." She spun on her heel and stalked off, but I was right behind her.

"Hey, what about our drink?"

"I'm sorry. I think it would be best if I just went home. This was a terrible idea."

I took Flynn's hand in mine and led her outside. I waited until I was sure we didn't have an audience before speaking.

"I don't know what the deal is with your brothers being surprised by your attire, but as I said earlier, I think you look really pretty."

"I don't usually wear stuff like this." Flynn waved her hand in front of her dress. "In fact, I never do."

"I wouldn't have guessed it." I took her hand and twirled her in a circle. The dress she wore looked like any I'd expect to see on a girl who was also wearing cowboy boots.

She played with one of the ringlets in her hair. "I don't ever do anything with my hair either."

"Now you're just teasing me."

Flynn shook her head. "I'm not. I'm the least girly-girl you'll ever meet."

I raised my eyebrows and shook my head. "I work for the CIA, sweetheart. I can guarantee you I've met plenty of women less 'girly' than you."

She looked away. "I had to go buy this dress today. I didn't have one."

"Flynn?"

"Yeah?"

"Let's go back in, get something to drink, and dance some more."

"I should just go home. I have to get up really early to start breakfast."

"One more dance. Please."

22

Flynn

I flopped down on the bed, unable to wipe the silly grin off my face. Tonight had been magical. The giddy feeling that warmed my body from head to toe would probably keep me awake all night, but I didn't care. Tomorrow I'd be floating on air.

For the first time in my life, a man noticed me, paid attention to me, held my hand, held me in his arms. While I'd hoped he might try to kiss me at some point, the fact that he hadn't, didn't damper my happiness.

The only thing that might've, if I'd allowed it to, were my brothers Porter and Cord. Was it really necessary for them to be so outwardly shocked that I was wearing a dress and comment on it no less?

Thankfully, all Holt did was find us to say hello in between his sets. And Buck—he was too distracted by Stella to even notice me.

The other thing I wouldn't allow to creep in was my insecurity. Paxon was probably just being nice, without any idea that tonight marked a kind of milestone for me, beyond what I'd told him about having to shop for something to wear. I'd never admit all the other things that had been firsts for me.

I ran my hands down the dress I didn't want to take off. The woman at the Gunnison Western Wear Store had been so kind to me. When I explained what I was looking for, she picked out several pieces for me to try on, and even though I was skeptical they'd fit when she showed me to the dressing room, every one had.

"Let me see," she'd said, smiling when I opened the door. "That one brings out the blue in your eyes. Try another one."

"Don't you have other customers you need to help?" I'd asked.

"Nope. We're slow today."

As much as I'd been tempted to buy them all, I left the store with only one. The saleslady said she'd keep the others in the back in case I changed my mind.

After the dress, she'd helped me pick out a new pair of boots, ones with embroidered flowers. "These are not work boots, young lady," she'd said with a wink.

I was getting ready to leave after I'd paid the bill when I heard her call out to me to wait. She followed me out, put a Be Right Back sign in the window, and took me three doors down to the salon.

"By the way, I'm Nina and this is Lucy."

"What are we here for today?" Lucy had asked.

"Just a little spruce up. Our friend is going to a CB Rice concert tonight."

"Oh, how fun! I wish I could go. Ben Rice is one fine-looking man." Lucy had put her hand on her heart. "What's your name, sweetheart?"

"Flynn."

"Come with me, Flynn, and we'll get those split ends cleaned up. How do you think you want to wear your hair tonight?" she'd asked, removing the ever-present hair tie.

Not only had she trimmed my hair, she curled it and showed me how to put on a little blusher.

"Your skin is so beautiful, you don't need makeup, but this will add a tiny bit of color to your cheeks."

When I told her I wasn't sure about buying the blusher, she threw it in with my haircut.

"You come back and tell me all about the concert," she'd said when she walked me to the door.

I wondered now if she really meant it or if she was just being nice too. I shrugged and rolled over, hugging my pillow tight and reliving every second of the night.

23

Irish

Why in the hell was my damn cell ringing so early in the morning? I was in the middle of the nicest dream about Flynn and resented the hell out of having to open my eyes.

"What?"

"Hey, Irish. It's Decker."

"I know that. What do you want?"

"I haven't been able to reach Buck or Stella."

"How is this my problem?"

"Paxon, come on. Go over there."

"You're fucking kidding me."

"I'll owe you one."

"You already owe me plenty." I hung up, pulled on a pair of pants and a shirt, stuck my feet in my boots, and traipsed next door.

"What can I do for you, Irish?" Buck asked after I pounded on the door long enough that I was about to break it down.

"Decker is trying to get in touch with you. Stella too. He finally called and asked me to walk over and see if you were both okay."

"Hey, Stella," Buck hollered.

She stuck her head out of the bedroom door. "Yeah?"

"As you can see, she's okay and so am I. Anything else?" asked Buck.

"He wants you to call him." I stormed back to my cabin.

A couple of hours later, I rubbed my eyes and closed my laptop. I wasn't accomplishing anything besides giving myself a headache. What there was to find on Kerr and his cohorts, I'd already found.

When I stood, I saw Buck and Stella come out of the cabin and leave with Rock. Why the hell hadn't Decker called him earlier and let me sleep? He was on Stella's detail.

It would probably be a shitty thing to call Flynn and tell her I needed something at the cabin, but I sure did want to see her.

"Hey, Ink. You somewhere close by?"

"Sure am. What do you need?"

"Have you eaten at the dining hall? Buck mentioned we were welcome to anytime."

"Hell yeah. There isn't any better food around that I know of."

"You hungry?"

He laughed. "I'm always hungry, Irish."

"How does this work?" I asked when we pulled up to a large building.

"It's basically cafeteria style, but the kitchen staff only plates stuff up as it's needed, so everything is fresh and hot."

Once inside, I looked around for Flynn but didn't see her. I followed Ink through the line, picking up a salad and then something that looked like a cheeseburger covered in something green.

"What's that?" I asked him.

"That's a slopper," I heard a woman's voice say. I looked over my shoulder and smiled at Flynn.

"I was hoping I'd see you today."

"You ever want to, I'm usually here."

"Tell me about the slopper. What's on top of it?"

"Green chili."

"Best I've ever had, but don't ever tell my mama," said Ink.

Flynn thanked him, grabbed a salad, and put it on a tray. "Mind if I join you?"

"I'd love it." I looked around when we got to the end of the food line. "Is there a cashier somewhere?"

Flynn laughed. "We don't charge for food."

"You don't?"

"It's part of the package for the staff, like the cowboys and hands. Obviously, it's included for paying guests." She shook her head. "Not that you're a paying guest. But you know what I mean."

I looked at her tray. "No slopper?"

"No, just a salad for me."

All three of Flynn's brothers looked up as we passed by their table. She kept going as if she didn't notice them, which was fine with me. Instead of sitting down with Ink, she went to an empty table.

"Is this okay?" she asked.

"Perfect." As she slowly nibbled on her salad, I dug into the mess on my plate. "Oh my God, what did you say this was?"

"First, tell me. Does that mean you think it's good?"

"Good? No. The best thing I've ever eaten in my life? Yes."

"All it is, is a cheeseburger covered in green chili. It's a Colorado thing."

I took a few more bites.

"There's more if you want another."

I raised my head and looked over to the food line. "I'd like ten more, but I better stop at one."

"The way you look, you could get away with having another one."

"The way I look?" I knew what she meant, but flirting felt so damned good, I kept it up.

Her cheeks flushed and she grinned, which was exactly what I was going for. "You know, you're very fit."

"And you are very pretty when you smile. You're pretty all the time, but especially then."

"Thank you," she murmured, but the smile left her face.

"Last night was fun," I said before finishing off the last of the slopper. "What else do you like to do when you're not working?"

Flynn looked away. "I'm always working."

"That can't be true."

She turned her head, and her eyes met mine. "It is."

"Come on now, you can't be here seven days a week."

"To be honest, before now, I haven't minded."

"What's different?"

Her cheeks were pink again, and she couldn't contain her grin.

"I like your dimples." Something about that compliment took her smile away again. I reached over and put my hand on hers. "What did I say wrong?"

She shook her head.

"Come on, tell me so I don't do it again."

"My face…"

"Is beautiful. What else?"

"It's pudgy." She stood and took my plate.

"I can do that."

"I know. I'm going to get you another slopper."

I grasped her wrist. "Flynn, don't run away from me."

"I'm not. I told you I'm getting you—"

"I can fetch my own food. Please sit back down."

When she did, I turned her chair so she was facing me. I reached up and was about to touch her face when I noticed her eyes darting around the room like I'd seen her do last night in the car. I pulled my hand away. The things I had to say to Flynn should be done without an audience.

"Can you take a break?"

"What for?"

"Maybe you could show me around Crested Butte?"

"Um, I probably shouldn't."

I heard someone clear their throat behind me and turned.

"Hey, Flynn, hey, Paxon," said one of her brothers I met the night before. I think it was Cord.

I nodded. "Hey."

"Holt is playing a show at the Goat tonight. Just him. They're shutting the place down, so it's family only and, uh, guests. If you want to go."

I looked back at Flynn. "I'd like to, would you?"

"Sure. That would be fun."

"Great. What time?" I asked.

"Not sure, but someone will let you know," said Cord.

I saw Ink get up and take his dishes and tray to a stand near a trash can.

"I guess I should head out since you have to work, but I'll see you later, right?"

24

Flynn

"Why did he say you had to work?" Cord asked when Paxon walked away. "You're done for the day."

"I still have to clean up and do prep for tomorrow."

"The kitchen crew can clean up, and I can do the prep. You can take time off, Flynn. In fact, if you don't start, we'll force you to."

"What does that mean?"

"It means you have four brothers who love and care about you, and you shouldn't be spending every waking moment in the dining hall."

"I like being here."

Cord motioned with his head to where Paxon stood, waving at us. "You like him?"

I was stunned at my brother's question and shrugged. "He's just being nice."

"Kinda old for you."

I swatted him. "I said he's being nice, is all."

"While I stand by what I just said about his age, if Paxon can get you to spend some time away from this place, then I think you should do it."

"What's going on?" asked Porter, who walked up with Holt.

"I'm just saying Flynn needs time off."

"I agree," said Porter.

"Same," said Holt. "You spend way too much time here. No one expects you to."

I felt my eyes filling with tears and turned my head away. It had always been easier to be here than go anywhere else. Mainly because I didn't have anywhere else to go, and if I did, no one to go with.

Porter put his hand on my shoulder. "We're not kicking you out of here, sis. We're just saying you work too much."

"Like the three of you don't?"

"I would agree that we all spend too much time on this ranch," said Cord. "In the past, the old man didn't give us much choice. Hard habit to break."

"Now's not the time for us to start planning vacations," said Porter. "I'll remind you, we have a deadline to get this place profitable or we lose it."

"Right," said Cord. "But that doesn't mean Flynn shouldn't be able to take a day or two off a week."

My eyes opened wide. "A day or two?"

"Yes," said Holt. "The staff knows your recipes. Cord can cover when you're not here."

I looked at Cord to see his reaction, but he didn't have one.

"Even if you're just not here. Go out, visit restaurants, see what people like to eat. Hell, get out of the valley. Go over to Buena Vista or Salida for a day. See if there's anything you want to add to the menu for the dude ranch guests."

"Speaking of dude ranch guests," said Porter. "I saw some of the guys working on the security system checking out the North Fork cabins."

"Why?" asked Cord.

"Dunno, but maybe you should find out."

When my brothers left, I wandered into the kitchen, realizing they were right about there not being anything for me to do.

After checking everything was set for the next day, I left. Normally, I would've hung out, tried out new recipes, or just puttered around. It was weird to leave and not have anything in particular to do.

Instead of going to the ranch house, I drove out of the Roaring Fork gates and went to Gunnison to see if Nina still had the dresses set aside for me.

"Hey, Flynn. Your brother was here earlier," she said when I walked in. "You're Buck's sister, right?"

"Right." I looked around the store. "Um, do you still have those dresses I tried on?"

She came around the counter. "Of course I do. That was just yesterday." She winked. "By the way, how was the concert? Lucy and I were so envious!"

I told her about it and that my brother played in the band. It felt weird to be telling so much to a stranger, but she was so friendly, I found myself jabbering away.

"After you left yesterday, I pulled a few more things for you to try on, if you're interested."

"Uh, sure. What kinds of things?"

She pulled on my belt loop. "Women's jeans for one. Something that will flatter your figure more. And some blouses that will do the same."

I followed her over to the dressing room area and waited while she went into the back. My eyes opened wide when I saw all the clothes she was carrying.

"Don't worry, you can just pick a couple of things, but at least you'll know what we have."

Once I graduated from high school, my father started paying me to run the kitchen. I knew it wasn't as much as he'd paid Johnny, but he'd also worked at the ranch for years.

Since I didn't do much, didn't have rent to pay, and hardly spent any money at all, I had enough in the bank to buy as many clothes as I wanted.

I thought about my conversations with my brothers and how I always worked, never did anything else, and decided that whatever I liked from what Nina had picked out for me, I'd buy.

I was pulling on a pair of jeans when I heard the chimes of the front door opening. A few seconds later, I heard Lucy holler at me.

"Hey, Flynn."

"You come out here and let us see," said Nina. "Lucy wants to hear about the concert too."

I spent two hours at the store, mainly chatting with the two women. I bought almost all the clothes Nina chose for me and some other things Lucy thought would look nice. I did have to reassure them more than once that I could afford it all.

When I told them my brother was playing a show at the Goat in Crested Butte, Lucy insisted she do my hair again, and since I had no idea how to fix it myself, I let her.

I left, promising I'd come into town next week and we'd all have lunch together.

Before I had a chance to start the truck, a call came in on my cell from Paxon. I held my breath, hoping he wasn't calling to say he didn't want to go tonight.

"Hi," I answered.

"Hey, Flynn. It's Irish. Sorry, um, Paxon."

"It's okay. I know they call you Irish."

"Anyway, I was just calling to see if you were still going tonight."

"I want to. Are you?"

"As long as you are."

I laughed. "Then, I guess we're both going."

"Sorry, I can be kind of an idiot sometimes." He sounded down, which threw me.

"Is everything okay?" I asked.

"Yeah, it's all good."

"You don't have to go tonight if you're not up for it."

"No, I'm looking forward to it. Really. I just wanted to make sure you were since we went to see a band last night."

"We're a pair," I said, laughing again at how we both kept reassuring each other.

"Bye, Flynn."

I stared at the phone when the call ended abruptly. Was it my imagination, or had he been short with me throughout the conversation? For a minute, I thought about going back in the store and returning all the clothes I'd just bought. It wasn't like tonight was a date. We were just two people going to see my brother play at a bar. I was making so much more of it in my head.

As Cord said, Paxon was too old for me, or maybe it was more that I just wasn't the kind of woman men would ever find attractive—even if I did buy a bunch of new clothes and have someone fix my hair.

When it was time to get ready, I was almost tempted to put on my "regular" clothes and pull my hair up in a ponytail but knew, if I did, it would make me feel worse, not better.

Instead, I picked a blouse that reminded me of the Icelandic poppies that filled the flower beds throughout Crested Butte. I pulled on a pair of new embroidered jeans and slipped my feet into the red booties Nina said would match the top perfectly.

I knew I should probably eat something since all I'd had today was a salad, but then my jeans would probably feel too tight and I'd be miserable.

"Hey, Flynn. You ready?" Cord called out to me.

"Yep."

"Wow," he said, looking me up and down when I came out of my room.

"What?"

"I like it. You look gorgeous, kid."

"Really?"

"Yes, really. Now let's go."

"Are we picking anyone else up?" I asked once we were in his truck.

Cord shook his head. "The secret service caravan is meeting us there I guess."

"It does kind of seem that way, doesn't it?"

"Do you ever wonder what the hell the big secret is?"

I shrugged. "I guess I'm used to it, given Buck could never talk about where he was or what he was doing."

25

Irish

"Aren't we picking anyone else up?" I asked Rock when we drove past the main ranch house.

"Everyone else is meeting us there."

I took a deep breath and let it out slowly, hoping I hadn't been so much of an asshole earlier that Flynn decided not to go along tonight. Evidently, I wasn't very good at separating work from fun since it had been so long since I'd done it. I was so accustomed to being wrapped up in the mission, I hadn't realized until I hung up that I'd probably given her the impression I wasn't interested.

But, Jesus, did I have any right to be interested? She was Buck's little sister, for God's sake.

"What's wrong?" asked Rock.

"Nothin'."

"Come on, now. Five minutes ago, you seemed almost happy. Now you're miserable again."

"It's been a long time since I've lived any kind of normal life. It isn't like I can, even now."

"Why not? Missions are missions. It doesn't mean we can't also be human every once in a while. Even you, Irish."

I breathed a sigh of relief when we walked into the bar and I saw Flynn seated at a table in the back. At least she'd come tonight and I hadn't ruined it for her.

Buck and Stella were sitting with her, as was Porter and a woman I didn't recognize.

"Hey," said Flynn, coming over to meet me at the bar.

"Hey there, can I get you a drink?" I asked.

"Um, sure. I'll have whatever you're having."

"Beer okay?"

"It's perfect."

"Can I see some ID?" the bartender asked.

Flynn reached into her pocket, pulled out a thin wallet, and handed him her license. "So embarrassing," she mumbled.

We'd just returned to the table with our beers when Holt stepped up to the mic, introduced himself, and played his first song. It wasn't long before Buck and Stella were dancing along with another couple.

"Who's that?" I asked.

"That's Ben Rice and his wife, Olivia. Don't you recognize him?"

"Should I?"

Flynn giggled. "We went and saw his band play last night."

"Nope, I didn't recognize him."

Flynn took a sip of her beer, stood, and held her hand out to me. "Wanna dance?"

The dance floor in the bar was a lot smaller than the one in the barn, but that was okay; we didn't move around too much.

I took a break to go to the men's room, and when I came back, I didn't see Flynn anywhere. I ordered another beer and turned around to watch Holt play. A flash of a red-print top caught my eye, and I realized Flynn was dancing with a guy I didn't remember meeting.

"Who's that?" I asked Buck when he came and stood next to me.

"You mean dancing with Flynn? That's Paco. He's one of the guys who works in the kitchen."

The bartender slid Buck's drinks across the bar while I watched Flynn dance with a man a lot closer in age to her than I was. Somebody who'd probably be sticking around longer than I would be too since he worked at her family's ranch.

Whatever the guy said to her made Flynn laugh. He tightened his arm around her waist, spun her around, and she giggled. Once she started, she couldn't stop. The guy was laughing too.

When her brother started another song, the two kept dancing.

"How's it going?" asked Ink.

"Pretty tired. Anybody heading to the ranch?"

"I can take you if you want."

"Don't want to spoil your fun."

Ink raised one eyebrow. "I'm on your detail, man. This isn't about fun."

I threw some money on the bar and left before the song ended.

* * *

Instead of going to the dining hall, I made do with what I had at the cabin for the next few days. When I needed something, I asked one of the guys to pick up whatever it was for me the next time they went into town.

I felt like a jerk both for my foolish flirtation with Buck's kid sister and for leaving the bar that night without saying a word to her. Both were jackass moves, but neither mattered. I was here to do a job while, at the same time, keeping my head down so I didn't draw attention or bring danger to the Roaring Fork.

There was no doubt that if our suspicions were right and we hadn't nailed everyone with the arrests of a couple of months ago, whoever was still out there would be gunning for not just me but Cope, Ali, and Decker too.

I still wasn't convinced that Stella's aunt, Kerr, or Interpol were connected to Fisk, but until we ruled that out, I had to consider it a possibility.

Something outside caught my eye, and when I stood, I saw it was Flynn. She dropped a package off on the porch and turned around to leave. From what I could tell, she kept her eyes down the whole time.

I raced over to the door, pulled it open, and called out her name. She turned around and shielded her eyes from the sun.

"Did you need something?"

"I wanted to talk to you for a minute."

"Is there something wrong with your cabin?"

"No, nothing like that. I just thought I should explain about the other night."

She opened the driver's door to her truck. "Nothing to explain. Have a good rest of your day, Paxon."

"Hang on."

Flynn got in the truck, but when I approached, she rolled the window down.

"You were having so much fun, and I didn't want to put a damper on your night."

"Yeah, your leaving didn't put a damper on my night at all."

"Like I said, it seemed as though you were having fun."

"Right. Was there anything else?"

"No. I just wanted to make sure things were okay between us."

"Yep." She turned her head and rolled up the window. As she drove away, I wondered if it was my imagination or if she had tears in her eyes.

* * *

It took three more days before I saw Flynn again, and in order to do so, I had to invent a reason.

"Your pilot light is out," she said, sitting up from where she lay on the floor, inspecting my stove. She stood, walked over to one of the drawers, and pulled out a long-handled lighter.

"Do you want me to do it?" I asked.

"If you could do it yourself, I wonder why you called me." She lay back down, reached in, and lit it. "There. You're all set."

When she stood up, I grasped her wrist and took the lighter from her hand. "I'm sorry."

"Not a big deal. Next time, you'll know what to do."

"That's not what I'm sorry for."

"I know."

"So you're saying the next time I'm at a bar with you, I'll know not to leave?"

"The next time you're at a bar with a woman you acted like you wanted to meet you there, my advice would be not to disappear on her. As far as with me, that won't be happening again."

"Flynn, please accept my apology."

"Accepted. Now, I need to get to work."

I looked beyond her and saw Buck approaching in his pickup followed by an SUV. When they both parked, I watched Cope and Ali get out of the second vehicle.

"Friends of yours?" asked Flynn, walking out the front door with me right behind.

"Yeah."

"I'll let you get to it, then. Bye, Paxon."

"Flynn, I'd really like to continue this conversation later."

"Yep," she said, waving behind her. I didn't think for a split second she intended to allow me to.

I hugged Ali and Cope and followed them into Stella's cabin, where Buck and Decker waited.

"Shall we get started?" asked Cope without any preamble whatsoever. He motioned for the rest of us to take a seat.

Decker looked at Buck, then me, and winked. He stood and cleared his throat. "Before we do that, you should know Stella is the lead on this mission. Anything related to the execution of it, has to be approved by her."

Cope's eyes opened wide. "Is Stella contracting for the Invincibles now?"

"That's right, and if this goes as well as I'm hoping and she's interested, we may offer her a permanent partnership. Her exceptional investigative skills are certainly worth adding to the team."

I wondered if Deck was serious or just blowing smoke up Cope's ass.

"Take a seat, Copeland," said Buck, turning to Stella. "Go ahead whenever you're ready."

I listened as Stella went over things I'd already heard or knew about. She told Cope and Ali how she'd gone to visit her aunt the day after their wedding and then found her dead a few days later.

I half listened as she continued the story about her aunt's career in journalism ending when she wrote an article accusing Nicholas Kerr, then-president of Interpol, of accepting bribes in the cover-up of Operation Argead.

She told them about the safe-deposit key her aunt had tried to give her that night and that Rock found hidden in her piano after she died.

Ali had questions about the evidence Stella's aunt allegedly had, but since no one knew where the safe-deposit box was located, there was no way to know what was in it.

"Why didn't she just release the evidence then if she had it?" Ali asked.

"They threatened to kill her." All eyes turned and looked at me.

"But why kill her now?" Ali asked.

"Exactly. Why now, instead of ten years ago?" asked Stella.

I looked at Decker. "You said there weren't any bugs in Barb's apartment. Is that right?"

"Affirmative," Deck answered.

It was obvious to me that either the bugs had been removed by whomever killed the aunt and her housekeeper, or the housekeeper was the one who'd ratted Barb out.

"What do we know about the other victim?" Ali asked, obviously thinking the same thing I was.

Stella told her that her aunt's caregiver had worked for Barb since shortly before the career-ending scandal, but she knew little about her, including whether she had any family.

"How did your aunt find her?" Ali asked.

"I can't remember the details, but I think it was through a temp agency."

Ali volunteered to see what else she could find out about the woman. "What's next?" she asked Stella.

"Irish, Buck, and I have been focusing on making connections between the people we consider to be players both back when Barb made the accusations and more recently. Let's start with Nicholas Kerr, Antoine Moreau, and Stanley Donofrio."

I'd been researching all three men extensively over the last several days.

"What are you thinking?" Stella asked me, perhaps noticing I was lost in thought.

"How many cold cases of murdered agents could be linked to these three men."

"And?"

"All of the older ones."

She continued to talk about her aunt, Kerr, and what she believed was a possible connection to Ed Fisk.

Judging by Cope's reaction, he thought it was as much of a stretch as I did.

What I was far more interested in was how Fisk might be connected to Interpol's current executive committee. I turned to Stella when she took a deep breath.

"You okay?" I asked.

She nodded and told Ali about Kerr's marriage to her aunt's former editor. "Clearly, they set her up."

"How?" asked Ali.

I cleared my throat, and Stella told me to go ahead. "I'm theorizing, but Kerr knew Barb had enough evidence to bring him down because Sally shared Barb's story with him. Neither of them thought anyone would pick it up. After it ran, Hennessey wrote the follow-up herself, and in it, accused Barb of manufacturing evidence."

"As well as accusing her of having an affair with Kerr that ended badly," Stella added.

"It makes sense that one or both of them threatened your aunt. Like Irish, I'm theorizing," said Buck. "Kerr, most likely, delivered the threat, demanding your aunt turn the evidence over to him or he'd kill her. She refused, but he didn't go through with it."

"Why not?"

"Mutually beneficial arrangement," said Decker, who had been mostly quiet to that point.

"Meaning?" asked Stella.

"She still had something on him. Probably whatever is in the safe-deposit box. And someone, like Barb's attorney for example, has instructions for what to do in the event of her untimely death."

"Wouldn't that come into play now?" asked Ali.

"Not if Kerr believed he could intercept it," Buck answered, stroking his beard.

"Because he finally knew where it was?" I asked.

"I still don't understand the timing," said Ali.

"There's a connection. I'm sure of it," I mumbled.

"Between?" Ali asked.

"The housekeeper and either Kerr or Hennessey."

"I need to find that damn safe-deposit box, and in order to do that, I need to go to New York and meet with Barb's lawyer," said Stella.

"Have you spoken with him?" asked Deck.

"Not since the first time."

"I'll check with the medical examiner and see if the death certificate is available yet. If it is, then I agree. If not, I'd recommend waiting."

Stella left the room. I assumed to call her aunt's attorney. My eyes met Cope's, and he motioned for me to join him outside. Before we got to the front door, Ali and Buck swept past us.

"We'll be back in a minute," she told Cope.

"What the hell is that all about?" I asked.

"Ali sticking her nose into Buck and Stella's business."

"Why?"

"My guess is she's not exactly thrilled that the two appear to be in a relationship."

"Does it bother you?"

Cope smiled and shook his head. "I'm not sure what you're asking me exactly, but I feel confident Buck will put my wife in her place."

"I meant that Ali and Buck are so close."

"Doesn't bother me at all. She's married to me, and based on what I've seen, Buck is with Stella."

"How is it, being married?"

Cope walked over and sat on the oversized sofa. I followed.

"All those years, I never would've believed it was possible. Ya know?"

"I do."

"And yet, here we are. What about you? Who was the woman I saw coming out of your cabin?"

"That's Buck's sister. She helps run what I think will eventually become a dude ranch. We're the first guests."

"Looked like there was more to it."

"To what?"

"The two of you."

"You're imagining things."

"It's okay, Irish."

I didn't want to have this conversation, but I knew Cope well enough to anticipate he wouldn't let it go. "We had a flirtation, and then I realized two things."

"What?"

"She's half my age, she's Buck's little sister, and as soon as I possibly can, I'm leaving."

"That's three things, and here's the way I see it. First, she isn't half your age unless she looks really old for seventeen."

"It would be eighteen, asshole, and she's twenty-one."

"So legal. Way beyond legal, actually."

"If three years is way beyond."

"Second, Buck didn't seem the slightest bit fazed when I asked who the woman was I saw coming out of your cabin."

"Because he knew she was delivering supplies."

"Right. And third,"—he waved his arm in the direction of the view—"this place is un-fucking-believably beautiful. Where are you in such a hurry to go?"

"I'd like to be a free man at some point in my life, Cope."

"I hear you there."

I looked over and saw Buck was back inside, talking to Decker, and Ali was head-to-head with Stella. "We should join them."

Cope got right to the point when we did. "I'm still not following how this directly connects to Fisk," he said. "Or how you're linking Kerr to Barb's murder."

"I located travel records indicating Kerr flew from London to New York City two days before Stella found Barb dead," I told him.

"I've been watching facial recognition feeds," added Decker. "So far, I haven't gotten any hits, but Kerr would know how to avoid being picked up."

"Are you saying we don't presently know Kerr's whereabouts?" Cope asked.

"That's correct," answered Decker. "Although we have reason to believe he hasn't left the States."

Cope stood and walked around the table. "Unless anyone here objects, I'm going to go to Money McTiernan with this." He turned to Stella. "That's if you truly believe your aunt has the evidence you think she does."

Stella's mouth opened and shut.

"Asshole," I muttered on her behalf.

"Well?" Cope asked.

"It's either in the safe-deposit box or whoever killed her took it," she said, standing and walking over to the window.

"I'm not involving Money unless we're sure."

Ali reached over and put her hand on her husband's arm. During Cope's original investigation, it was Money who'd brought in Ali, a CIA internal affairs officer, to determine whether Cope was also a double agent working with me.

Once Money found out the nature of the mission we'd conducted on our own and that we suspected Fisk of leading a ring of double agents responsible for the deaths of some of the CIA's best operatives, he backed us with the full force of the agency, all under the auspice of internal affairs—which was how he was able to hide it from Fisk. Not to mention with support from the Senate Intelligence Committee, chaired by none other than Cope's father, Henry Clay Copeland, Senior Senator from the State of Louisiana.

I knew none of this at the time, of course.

If Cope planned to take this to Money, it had to also mean he hoped to secure funding to keep the mission going—something his senator father would certainly approve.

"No objections?" Cope asked. When no one spoke up, he continued. "Deck, err...and Stella, do you have the next steps determined?"

Stella looked at me.

"What?" I asked.

"What happened with China?"

"What about them?"

"You were on trial for spying for them. Was that part of the cover?"

I looked at Cope and then Deck. "They're pretty easy to make a scapegoat for just about anything," I said.

"To confirm, there was never an official connection to China?"

"Nothing concrete enough to base a case on. That doesn't mean they weren't somehow involved," said Cope, putting her off as easily as I had. It had become second nature to us both. Our suspicions about China, and maybe even Saint and Dr. Benjamin, hadn't changed, but like he said, we couldn't make a strong enough connection to do anything about it.

We talked more about Interpol's current executive committee, agreeing to continue researching their backgrounds as well as their known affiliations in intelligence.

I felt a migraine coming on. I'd give anything to return to my cabin and sleep. When I closed my eyes momentarily and thought about it, I realized that more than sleep, I wanted to see Flynn.

26

Flynn

I had absolutely no reason to feel guilty about the conversation I'd had with Paxon earlier, but I did. I drove up to the cabins, but one of the men standing watch told me the meetings were still going on.

I noticed one of the other guys near the grill. "Do you need any help with that?" I asked, walking over to see what he was cooking.

"We've got steaks, chops, and chicken."

"What are you serving with it?"

The man at the grill looked at the other guy, and they both shrugged.

"Tell you what, I'll go to the dining hall and bring back some stuff to go with all that meat."

I was loading everything when my cell buzzed with a text.

I'm sorry I screwed up.

Reading Paxon's words almost brought me to tears. He'd tried to apologize several times, and while I'd said I accepted it, I really hadn't. And why not? I was dancing with another guy when he left—even if it was just Paco, who was practically like another brother to me. If he'd done the same thing to me, I probably would've left too.

I'm sorry I screwed up too, I texted back.

You're forgiven.

So are you. BTW, I'm on my way there now.

Can't wait to see you.

When I walked in, our eyes met, and we both smiled. I wished so much that I could sit down and eat with them or, better yet, that he and I could leave and go someplace we could talk.

I'd just gotten to the dining hall when my cell phone rang.

"Where'd you run off to?" Paxon asked.

"You looked busy."

"Not busy anymore."

"No?"

"I was hoping we could talk, Flynn."

"I'd like that. Where?"

"Easiest if you come to me. If you don't mind."

I was in my work clothes, my hair was its usual mess, and I probably smelled like potato salad. "Give me an hour?"

"See you then."

27

Irish

There was no question whether what I was about to do was a bad idea. I already knew it was a terrible one, but Flynn needed to understand why I reacted in certain ways to certain things and to realize my foul moods had nothing to do with her.

"Hi," I said when she knocked on the cabin door and I invited her in.

"Hi."

"You look nice." Her cheeks flushed and she thanked me. When I offered her something to eat or drink, she refrained from both. I'd cracked open a beer right before she arrived and poured it into a glass.

"Thanks for coming over," I said, motioning for her to take a seat on the sofa.

"Is whatever you're about to tell me something bad?" she asked.

I took a deep breath and let it out slowly. "It's more fact than bad."

Flynn folded her hands on her lap. "Okay."

"Nine years ago, I watched three agents die when they were gunned down during what should've been a routine op."

Her eyes were wide. "I'm so sorry."

"When it happened again and the agency's response didn't make any sense to me, I began an investigation of my own. What I discovered was there were too many similar happenings."

"I'm just going to get a glass of water," she said, standing.

"I won't go on if this is making you uncomfortable."

"It isn't that. I just need a drink."

"I can't tell you how often I say the same thing when this topic of conversation comes up."

She smiled and sat down on the sofa after setting her glass on the coffee table. "Go on. I'm sorry I interrupted."

"As I was saying, the agency's response baffled me. In each case, the mission during which the agents were killed was swept under the carpet as if it never happened. Which, of course, made me suspicious. Cope was my handler at the time, so I eventually went to him, and for several years, he and I conducted an investigation outside of the agency and without the agency's permission."

"Is that why you were arrested?"

I shook my head. "No, that was a planned part of the mission, one intended to throw the real double agent or agents off in the hope they would act again and we would catch them."

"Did that happen?"

"To a certain extent, yes. What we discovered right before we arrived here at your family's ranch is that while many of the people who were involved had been arrested, there were still more out there who haven't been."

"Okay."

"Stella is an investigative journalist who may have a lead on the rest of the players. We're here because it is a safe place for us to continue trying to find the rest of the perpetrators as well as figure out what was behind the deaths. With every day that goes by and we don't do that, more agents' lives are at risk."

"And you feel personally responsible for that."

Her intuitive response didn't surprise me. "That's right, and there are times when it consumes me. It's impossible for me to separate myself from this mission in order to have what anyone might consider a normal life."

I turned my body so I was facing her. "Do you have any questions so far?"

"Not really. I'm used to Buck not being able to talk about his work."

"This is more about me personally than work, Flynn. I want you to understand why I've been inconsistent with you. I think you're very pretty, you're intelligent, and I enjoy spending time with you."

"But?"

"I have no business getting into any kind of relationship with anyone."

She scooted forward on the sofa.

"Please don't leave."

She nodded but didn't scoot back.

"I'd really like for us to be friends. I'd like to spend time with you when we're both not working, but I need you to understand that friends is all we can ever be and that has nothing to do with how much I may want more."

"I really need to go." When she stood, I saw tears in her eyes. I stood too and pulled her into an embrace.

"I'm sorry. I truly am. I'd like to say that once this is over, I may be able to think about relationships, but I sometimes wonder if it will ever be over."

Flynn took a step back and wiped her tears. "I feel like a real idiot for crying."

"Don't. I cry too."

She smiled. "Thank you for being honest with me."

"Whoever your next relationship is with, he will be a lucky man."

When she scoffed, I figured now wasn't the time to ask why.

"I meant what I said about us being friends. If you need someone to talk to or just feel like hanging out, I'd like to see more of you."

"I'd like that."

"Promise?"

"Yes."

"Good, because…I'm going to have a couple of days off and was wondering if we could plan some things."

"Like what?"

"How do you feel about horseback riding?"

She laughed. "Feel about it? That's like asking how I feel about walking or breathing; it's just something I do."

"I never have."

"I could make arrangements for you."

"Will you be with me?"

Flynn rolled her eyes. "Yes, Paxon, I'll be with you."

Going off the ranch was harder because of my detail, but we were able to schedule dinner after our ride the next day. The one where I made an absolute jackass out of myself. My self-deprecation over not being able to control the horse—the most mild-mannered one they had, according to Flynn—resulted in her getting the giggles more than once.

"Would you mind if we went somewhere a little farther away to eat tonight?" she asked when we returned the barn.

"Not at all. Where are you thinking?"

"There's a drive that goes from Crested Butte over Kebler Pass toward Aspen. There's a restaurant near the top in a place called Redstone. It's also a beautiful drive."

"Sounds good to me."

We left at four even though our reservations were at six, just so we could take our time and enjoy the scenery. Ink and one of the other contractors went with us.

"This is the largest grove of aspens in the world," Flynn said when we drove beneath the miles-long canopy of trees.

"I bet it's spectacular in the fall."

She beamed. "Nowhere else in the world is better."

I couldn't help but wonder if I'd ever have the opportunity to see it. Part of me hoped I'd be long gone by autumn because our mission was finally over. Another part hoped I'd still be here.

It didn't take long to get to Redstone, so we decided to take a walk on one of the trails before dinner.

"Are there any bears around here?" I asked when we were a quarter mile into our hike.

"You really aren't much of an outdoorsman, are you?" Flynn asked.

"Not so much."

"To answer your question, yes, there are black bears in these mountains; however, they usually keep their distance, and so do we."

With Ink leading the way and the other guy following, I doubted any bear would be able to get to Flynn or me, which made me wonder if shooting them was legal.

We didn't see many people on the trail. In fact, just one, but there was something about the way the guy, who appeared to be in his twenties, looked at Flynn that I didn't like. What's more, she reacted.

"Is that someone you know?" I asked when I believed we were far enough away that he wouldn't hear me.

"Just someone I went to high school with."

"I take it he wasn't a friend."

"No one was," she mumbled. "Can we change the subject?"

None of us said anything for quite a while, not that the two bodyguards would have. Finally, when we reached a clearing and I saw there was a small lake, I asked if we could sit for a minute.

When I believed Ink and his teammate were far enough away that we could talk privately, I asked what she meant.

"High school wasn't a fun time for me. I didn't have a lot of friends. Actually, I didn't have any friends."

"Why not?"

"I was bullied a lot." She took a deep breath and stood. "I'd rather not talk about it."

"We don't have to." I looked at the time. "Should we head back?"

Flynn didn't answer, but she did walk toward the trail.

Given we were going downhill rather than up, it took us half the time to get back to the inn and resort where the restaurant was. We were still an hour early, so I went inside to see if we could bump up our reservation. From the hostess' stand where I waited, I could see the guy we'd passed in the woods working behind the bar. I hoped his being here wouldn't ruin Flynn's evening, given she'd had such a strong reaction to seeing him.

"I have a table out on the veranda if you'd like. Are there four of you dining with us this evening?" the woman asked, looking out to where Ink waited with Flynn.

"Just two."

As I'd anticipated, Flynn stiffened when she saw the bartender. I'd intentionally walked between her and the bar, not that it helped.

We were the only diners in the place this early, so when the man said, "Hey, heifer," under his breath, I could hear him loud and clear. Based on her reaction, she did too.

"What did you just say?" I asked the man.

"Paxon, don't," Flynn whispered.

I might've done as she asked if the guy hadn't come around the bar. "I recognize you from the news. You're the guy they arrested for spying for China."

Ink moved closer while Flynn grabbed my arm and pulled me in the opposite direction and out of the restaurant.

"Figures the cow would hang out with the likes of you."

When Flynn flinched as though someone had physically assaulted her, I spun around on the guy and drew my hand back to punch him, but Ink got between us.

"Out," he said to me under his breath. "I'll handle this. You get Flynn to the SUV."

I did as he asked, knowing that if I ignored him, I'd only be making his job more difficult.

Flynn put her face in her hands once we were in the vehicle. "I'm so sorry."

I pulled her hands away. "You have nothing to be sorry for."

"I ruined dinner."

"You didn't ruin anything. The asshole guy behind the bar did."

"Can we please just go?"

I saw Ink on his way to the car. I'd ask him later what happened with the bartender. Flynn already felt bad enough.

I suggested we eat somewhere in Crested Butte when we came down the mountain and drove through town, but Flynn said she'd lost her appetite and just wanted to go back to the ranch.

I wished there was something I could do to make her feel better, but the harder I tried, the more she retreated into herself.

When a few days passed without my being able to reach her, I asked Buck about it when he came over to my cabin about something else.

"I don't know much about Flynn's high school friends since I'm so much older than her. Holt might, though."

"Why'd you stop over?"

"Right. Burns Butler is next door and wants to brief you and Cope on something."

Nothing could've prepared me for what the man told us.

28

Flynn

It was all I could do to come out of my bedroom, let alone get dressed and go to the dining hall. What I really wanted to do was disappear into a black hole, never to be seen again.

I'd never been so humiliated in all my life, even when it happened every day at school.

Paxon heard that asshole Trent call me a heifer. Every time I thought about it, I was sick to my stomach. Trent had made it even worse by saying he recognized Paxon from the news.

Why had I suggested we go to Redstone? That was an easy answer; because I'd thought there'd be less chance of running into someone I knew. Of course, the opposite would happen. Not only had we seen someone I knew, but that person had to open his mouth and let all the ugly shit I'd grown up with spew out of it.

Paxon had tried to contact me several times, but I ignored him. I didn't want to talk about that night. I wanted to forget it had ever happened. Talking to him, seeing him, would only remind me of my utter embarrassment.

29

Irish

When Cope and I went inside, Stella, Buck, and Burns were sitting in the living room. Decker was patched in via video-conferencing on one of their computers.

"It's a pleasure to meet you, sir," I said to Burns, reaching out to shake his hand.

"It's an honor, Mr. Warrick," he responded. "I've learned of your bravery from our friend Mr. Ashford. Yours as well," he said to Cope.

"Where is Ali?" Decker asked him.

"Lying down. She isn't feeling well." Both he and I looked back at Burns when he cleared his throat.

"I believe what you're about to read may hold some of the information you've been seeking."

Buck handed Cope an envelope that he passed to me. "You go first," he said. Before opening it, I looked up at Stella, who appeared hopeful.

The bulk of the report was about Kim Ha-joon, the South Korean secretary-general of Interpol, who wasn't South Korean at all. The name he was currently using was one of several known aliases. His given name was

Chen Wang-Su, and his father had worked in Chinese intelligence for many years. He was a known associate of Ming Shen-Lin—a Hong Kong citizen infamous in intelligence circles and rumored to be a double agent if not triple.

It came as no surprise to me that China would maneuver one of their spies into Interpol, only that it took us so long to figure it out.

I felt a sense of relief at knowing that China was involved. This was the proof. I wasn't crazy or paranoid or grasping at straws, not that anyone had ever suggested those things. I'd wondered it myself.

"As Buck said earlier, the current Interpol executive team knows exactly who he is," said Decker.

Burns leaned forward. "This serves as nothing more than a warning." He looked directly at me. "You, better than anyone in this room, understand the risks involved in continuing to pursue what we all now know to be Operation Argead. The global reach of this organization is infinite, and they are backed by the most powerful nations in the world, each with their own agenda."

"Understood, sir."

When Burns stood, I did too. "Come with me."

I followed him out to the porch, where Ink waited in one of the SUVs.

"When this is over, I'd like to invite you to visit me at Butler Ranch."

"I'd be honored, sir."

"I'll put you under advisement that my wife, Sorcha, will want every last detail about your mission, but she will reward you with some of the best food you've ever eaten, not to mention my son and daughter-in-law's wine."

Hearing those words from Burns, a man I'd admired from a distance the entirety of my career, buoyed me as I went inside after thanking him.

As I closed the door behind me, I saw Decker's computer screen go dark. There was too much tension in the room for it to have been him ending the video chat.

"What's going on?"

"All Decker said was that he received word from Casper that something had gone down."

Within a few minutes, he called back. "I don't have all the details, but it's bad. I'm leaving for Ireland now. I'll be in touch after I've assessed the situation."

"Do you need backup?" Buck asked.

"I'll engage Rile and see who we've got over there."

Two days later, we still hadn't heard from Decker with an update about what was happening in Ireland, but a nasty storm had moved into the Crested Butte area, causing flooding throughout the valley where the ranch was located. Fortunately, there had been no damage reported to any of the Roaring Fork structures, at least as of yet.

Somewhere in the back of my mind, I knew it was the Fourth of July, just like I knew when other holidays came and went. It had been so long since I'd celebrated any of them, I anticipated today would go like every other.

"Hey, Buck," I said when I answered his call in the late afternoon.

"My brothers and sister are serving dinner in the dining hall tonight. I also heard my brother Holt might be playing a set later."

"If you're calling to invite me, I'm going to take a pass on this one."

"You okay, Irish?"

"No different than usual."

"Sure I can't change your mind?"

"No. I'm good. I have a couple of leads I'm following."

"Need any help?"

"I'll let you know if I do."

I'd lost track of time when my cell rang again, this time with a call from Decker.

"Are you all together? I'd rather only do this once."

"Negative, but we can be."

"Call me when you are."

I immediately called Cope, who reported he saw Buck and Stella return to the cabin a couple of hours ago. When I came out the door, he and Ali were waiting for me.

"How are you feeling?" I asked her.

"Hanging in there." She rubbed her belly like maybe it had been a stomach bug.

"I got a call from Ashford. Something went down in Ireland. He asked if we were all together, and I told him I'd let him know when we were," I explained once we were inside Stella's cabin.

I opened my laptop and sent a message to Decker. Seconds later, he appeared on the screen.

"First of all, Byrne is dead, along with three of his henchmen," he began. "There was a hostage situation that culminated in us eventually finding a box that held the evidence he was after."

"Which was?" asked Cope.

"Nothing that referenced Operation Argead or linked him to anyone from Interpol, past or present."

Cope looked as though he was about to speak again, but shut his mouth when the rest of us in the room glared at him.

"What we did learn is somewhat shocking. Do you all remember the reporter Veronica Guerin? Turns out she wasn't investigating drug gangs as was reported at the time. She was part of a task force working on exposing corruption within the Irish Military Intelligence. The rest of the members of the unit, save three, were killed within a week of her death."

"What happened to the other three?" Ali asked.

"Irish?" said Decker.

I immediately knew the answer. "Special Agents Pierre Martin, Leon Schmidt, and Alan Perry. They were all murdered in La Chapelle-Saint-Maurice."

"The father of the agent I mentioned the other day, Siren Gallagher, was one of the men from the task force who was murdered," said Decker. "Byrne kept track of her all these years, thinking she might have evidence related to the crimes. Turns out, her mother, who passed away a few years ago, had it in a box that was supposed to be given to Siren but wasn't located until after Byrne's death."

Decker continued. "Stella, my contact in the Hays County Coroner's Office said the DC medical examiner is getting ready to release your aunt's death certificate. As soon as that happens, I think you should press to get a meeting scheduled with the attorney."

"I'll do that."

"Decker, Stella received something in the mail that was forwarded to her. It was a note from her aunt, sent the day Stella found her."

"What's in it?"

"We haven't been able to decipher its meaning."

"Send it to me. It'll give me something to do on the flight home."

"Roger that."

"Anything else I need to know before I get in the air?" Deck asked.

When no one spoke up, he ended the call.

"Can I see the note?" I asked.

Buck picked it up from the table and handed it to me.

Its message seemed obvious, given Barb's use of numbers. "What's at 610 Fifth Avenue?"

Buck pulled out his phone. "Tiffany's flagship store."

I took a photo of the note and told them I'd send it to Decker.

When I walked out, I saw Flynn's truck pulling up. I'd tried to reach her several times, and she hadn't responded. Since it was pouring rain, I didn't bother stopping to ask why not.

30

Flynn

I felt horrible when I saw Paxon leave the cabin we were about to go into and head next door. By the time I got out of the SUV, he was already inside.

Earlier, we thought everyone was coming to the dining hall, where we'd made a feast for the Fourth of July, but Stella had some mail delivered to the house, which I forgot to tell her about. Evidently, there was something important in it because both Buck and Stella left right after they got it.

I had no idea if Paxon had intended to come or not.

"Hurry up," yelled Cord, when I hesitated following them. It had been raining hard all day and hadn't let up. I grabbed two of the containers and raced inside.

"We brought food," I said when Buck opened the door.

"Best brisket ever," said Cord as he uncovered the large pan he brought inside.

"We were so busy in the kitchen that we didn't get a chance to eat," said Porter, coming in behind Holt, who brought his guitar along. "Mind if we eat with you?"

While I was a little sad at the thought that Paxon was all alone next door, I couldn't remember a time I'd had so much fun with my brothers.

We talked about our futures and plans for the ranch now that our dad was gone. Cord and I both wanted to see if we could make a go of the dude ranch, Porter wanted to get into the roughstocking business, and Holt obviously wanted to tour with CB Rice.

Buck didn't say much, but when Stella told us they'd talked about living in our great-grandparents' old farmhouse, a sense of peace came over me. It just felt right, and I said so. When Buck's eyes met mine, I knew in my heart that while it was hard for him to admit it, given his history with our dad, he felt the rightness of it too.

When it came time for us to go, I packed up a small amount of the food to take over to Paxon. I'd planned to leave it for him, but when I walked up to the cabin, I saw him sitting on the swing.

"How come you're sitting in the dark?" I asked.

He shrugged. "I guess I didn't plan on staying out here that long."

"I brought you some food."

"That was nice of you." He held out his hand.

"I can take it inside."

"Thanks."

The lack of enthusiasm in his voice made me so sad. I went back out and sat beside him on the swing. This was one instance where I was glad we were sitting in the dark.

"I was so embarrassed," I said.

"I know. I was too."

"I'm sorry you had to experience that. It's why I've stayed away."

"Do you know why I was embarrassed?"

I shrugged.

"Because he recognized me. I saw that same look I've seen on the faces of so many people. I'm sorry you had to witness that."

"You've done nothing wrong, though."

"Have you?"

"It's different."

Irish put his arm on the back of the swing. "You're sorry I had to witness someone shaming you, right?"

"Who would want to hang around with someone who gets called a heifer?"

"Who would want to hang around with someone who gets called a traitor?"

"But you aren't."

He drew me into him. "And neither are you, Flynn."

My eyes filled with tears, and when he put his other arm around me, I let myself sink into his embrace.

"I wish I could take all your hurt away," he whispered.

"I wish I could take yours away too."

"You know what works?"

"What?"

"For me, anyway, spending time with you. You have a way about you that soothes me, Flynn. I smile more. I don't think about the dark stuff as much."

"I feel the same when I'm with you."

"If that's the case, why aren't we spending more time together?"

Even in the dark, I could tell he was smiling.

"We should be," I said, resting my head on his shoulder.

31

Irish

Two days later, Buck and Stella were on their way to New York City, where they hoped to find the location of her aunt's safe-deposit box.

Because of something in his father's will, Buck couldn't be away from the ranch for more than forty-eight consecutive hours, or he and his siblings would lose their inheritance. I didn't understand it—at all—and said so when Flynn tried to explain it to me. All I knew was that Hammer, the attorney the Invincibles kept on retainer, said it was legal and binding.

What that meant was they had forty-eight hours to fly to the East Coast, find the safe-deposit box Stella believed contained evidence regarding Operation Argead, gather that evidence together, and fly back. I hoped it would be that easy, but I doubted very much it would be.

I was getting ready to text Flynn to see if she had free time later in the day to get together, when Cope knocked on the cabin door. When I opened it, he pushed past me, carrying his open laptop.

"You are not going to fucking believe this." He set the laptop down on the table.

"What?"

"Look for yourself."

"China has granted US whistleblower Xander Harris permanent residency rights," began the intelligence bulletin.

"Who the fuck is Xander Harris?"

"Keep reading."

The report mapped out Harris' timeline beginning when his father was deployed to the Gulf War. Xander, given name William, was eight at the time. His father was deployed again to Afghanistan when Xander was sixteen.

Right out of college, paid for with his father's GI Bill, Xander secured a job working for the US government as an IT and cybersecurity tech.

I looked up at Cope. "Has Decker seen this?"

He pulled out his phone while I continued reading.

Two years after Harris was hired, his father committed suicide outside of a VA hospital, after reportedly being denied care for Gulf War Syndrome and PTSD.

Three months later, he left his job with the government and went to work for Enigma Computers, based in Hawaii.

"That name sounds familiar. Why?"

Cope shrugged. "Decker is on his way here now. He should land in about an hour. And to answer your earlier question, he's read the bulletin."

"Is that why he's on his way?"

"Affirmative."

I continued reading. Nine years ago, Xander Harris relocated from Hawaii to Hong Kong.

I sat back in the chair. "Holy fucking shit."

"What?"

I pointed to the paragraph of the bulletin that referred to the timing of Xander's relocation from Hawaii to Hong Kong. "Cope, do you think…"

"I know what you're going to say, and I'm as hopeful as you are."

"But?"

"Cautiously hopeful."

"There's still a matter of how this relates to what Stella's aunt may have uncovered."

"If that amounts to anything."

"Have we always been this negative?" I asked.

"Maybe not nine years ago. I don't know. Maybe we're just realistic."

"Hey, where's Ali?" It dawned on me that Cope had been here close to thirty minutes.

"Lying down. She's…uh…not feeling well."

Obviously, there was something more to it I was missing, but right now, I had more important things to be concerned with.

I dove as deep as I could into William "Xander" Harris' background, which was like diving into a quarter inch of water. "Fisk buried him," I said, assuming Cope wasn't finding any more than I was.

"China calls him a 'US whistleblower,' but I can't find anything whatsoever about what he blew on."

"Maybe we'll have better luck once Deck gets here."

A few minutes later, we heard him before we saw him. "Goddamn motherfucking sonuvabitch. I grew up on a ranch; you'd think I'd know to be on the lookout for horse shit."

I went out on the porch where he was scraping his boot on the step.

"Hey, Irish."

"Hey, Deck."

He stormed past me, threw his laptop on the table more than set it, and pulled a chair out.

"We got anybody close enough to China to get in and kill this little motherfucker?"

I looked at Cope, who was looking at me.

"Yes, Rile, I am serious."

Only then did we realize he was talking on his cell, although I didn't see it, nor did I see any kind of earpiece. Then again, this was Decker we were talking about. Maybe he had something implanted in his brain that allowed him to simply make a call by thinking it— or some other shit only he'd dream up.

Decker sat down, took a deep breath, and rested his hands on the edge of the table. "Something tells me this is our mole."

I nodded, and so did Cope.

"The question is, how do we tie him to Kerr?"

"Our thoughts as well."

"I gotta tell you, fellas, I'm thinking about reading Doc Butler in on this."

"You don't think he already knows?"

Deck's eyes met mine. "You mean via Burns?"

"Yes."

"Fuck no," he spat, shaking his head.

Burns was Doc's father; was it really so hard to think he'd discuss Operation Argead with his son? Evidently so.

"As far as reading Doc in, would anyone object?" Cope asked.

"Anyone whose opinion I give two shits about? Nope," answered Decker.

When he stood and walked over to the window, seemingly on another call, I wondered again about the brain-implant thing. How the hell had he done it otherwise?

"Doc, Decker here. How soon can you and your team get to Colorado?"

There were a few seconds of silence. "Yeah, I know you have a fleet of planes now, asshole. Just answer the question. How soon?"

The next thing I heard was him asking Rile the same thing. "Yes, this supersedes my directive to kill the little bastard."

Decker returned to the table and sat down. "How's Ali feeling?" he asked.

"Still pretty rough."

"It'll pass," said Decker.

"Do you want to elaborate as to what you're talking about?"

Decker ignored me, and Cope looked at me as if I were an idiot.

"What?"

"She's pregnant, asshole," Decker said before Cope could. "Now, can we get back to business?" He looked between the two of us, and I nodded.

"The way I see it, we may have two investigations to conduct. First is to figure out who the hell this Harris guy is, what and how much he's given to China, and who else he's connected to. At the same time, we need to determine whether this weasel has anything to do with Argead or if the two are unrelated. Then we meet in the middle."

"Copy that," both Cope and I responded.

"Irish." He turned his chair so he was facing me. "Both teams report to you." He looked over his shoulder at Cope. "As do you."

"Roger that."

"Good. Now, I'm going to ask one more thing of you."

"Go ahead."

"I want you to make Stella the lead on the Kerr side of things."

"Roger that," I repeated.

"No objections?"

"Isn't that what she is now?"

"What we've been working on for the last few weeks is a flea on a dog compared to the horse we've gotta break now." He looked between Cope and me. "No comment?"

"About the analogy?"

Decker laughed and pointed his thumb at Cope. "Is he really this much of a pussy?" he asked me.

"Not even a little bit."

His eyes scrunched, and the smile left his face. "I'm damn glad to hear it, Irish."

"News out of DC isn't good, boys," said Decker, looking at his phone several hours later. "Stella got the runaround today when she met with the attorney who took over after Barb's lawyer was murdered, so she still hasn't located the safe-deposit box. Worse, they found evidence that the housekeeper had been working for Kerr for years. Some relation to his wife."

"And Kerr killed her?" asked Cope.

"If, in fact, he was the killer, then yes, it would appear that way."

"How's Stella doing?" I asked.

"She's okay, Irish. I'm sure she'd appreciate hearing from you directly, though."

I ignored his suggestion. I wasn't quite ready for Stella and I to be "buds."

The news didn't get any better the following day. While Stella and Buck had figured out where the safe-deposit box was located, the branch manager of the bank was demanding a warrant for her to get into it. On top of that, the storm that had flooded the valley where the Roaring Fork Ranch was located had moved to the East Coast, wreaking havoc on travel. Even if they managed to get the box's contents, now there was a question of whether they'd be able to return to Colorado in time to meet Buck's curfew.

"How serious is Buck's father's will?" I asked Decker.

"According to Hammer, if Buck doesn't follow it to the letter, the ranch will be sold and all the assets, including the proceeds from the sale, will be given to charity."

"Seems extreme," I mumbled.

"Extreme? Seems downright vengeful, bordering on psychotic, if you ask me."

I was glad Decker said it because that was really more what I was thinking. I wondered how Flynn was doing and whether she even knew her brother was in danger of not making it back in time.

"I need to take a break," I said, heading out to the porch to call her.

She sounded tired when she answered. "Hey, Paxon."

"Hey, Flynn. I just wanted to check in with you. Things with the investigation have heated up. I anticipate working some long hours over the next few days, but I wanted you to know I was thinking about you."

"I was thinking about you too, Paxon."

"Yeah?"

"Yep."

"I sure wish we could sit on my porch swing and talk again tonight."

"I wish we could too. Listen, I have to go, though."

"Everything okay?"

"I'm not sure yet. My brothers have called a family meeting. We might have to find a way to cover up the fact that Buck might not make it back within forty-eight hours."

"I wondered if you'd heard."

"Maybe we can talk later?"

"I'd like that."

"How is she?" Decker asked when I came inside.

"If you've got my phone bugged enough to know who I was talking to, why is it you don't know what we discussed?"

Decker laughed. "I know you were talking to Flynn by the look on your face, Irish. I don't need any fancy spyware to read you like a book."

"He's smitten."

I glared at Cope, stunned he would say something like that. "We're friends."

"Right," both he and Decker said at the same time.

The next afternoon, we sat glued to our computers and phones, waiting for word from the East Coast. Buck returning to the ranch in forty-eight hours became the least of anyone's worries when we were alerted that both Rock and Ink were down and Stella had been kidnapped—not in DC, as we'd thought; it all went down in New York City.

Finally, Decker managed to reach Jinx Jenkins, who, even though he was chief of the DC Metro Police, was on the scene in New York. Decker put the phone on speaker.

"Johnson, Ryan, and TJ are fine. Nicholas Kerr is dead, as are the crew that nabbed her. I'm going to need a little help, Decker. First of all, I have no jurisdiction in the State of New York. Second, even if I did, cleaning up this mess would have the media in a frenzy."

"Jinx, you said you're on the scene?" Decker asked.

"Affirmative."

"What's the twenty on Stella and Buck?"

"Your whole team is on their way to the airfield."

"Copy that. Help is on the way."

When Decker ended the call, he looked at Cope. "How many cleaners can you get to New York City, and how fast?"

"How many do you need?"

"I'd say at least five. More would be better."

"You got it." Cope was about to make a call, but Deck held up his hand.

"You goin' official on this one?"

"Affirmative."

"Money McTiernan?"

Cope shook his head. "My dad."

Decker chuckled. "Knew he'd be good for somethin'."

Prior to the mission we undertook, Cope's father was more of a liability to his son's career. Since we read him in on our investigation last year, when both Cope and I almost died, the man's role as chair of the Senate Intelligence Committee had proved to be a valuable asset.

Decker got up again and walked toward the window.

"How the hell is he getting these calls?" I asked Cope. He shrugged.

Seconds later, Decker returned. "That was Buck. Unfortunately, the only thing in the safe-deposit box was another key. However, this time, Stella believes she knows what it's for. Once they land, they'll make a pit stop here and then head out again."

"Where to this time?" I asked.

"Back to New York City."

"What a clusterfuck," I muttered, thinking not just about the time that was being wasted but also the jet fuel. I was sure, though, that if there were any kind of loophole in Buck's father's will, Hammer would've found it.

I sent a text to Flynn when we agreed to call it a night. She probably already knew about her brother, but I'd tell her anyway, just in case she didn't.

Heard Buck and Stella are on their way back, I wrote.

Me too. So relieved, she responded.

I sat and stared at the phone, not knowing what else to say. I was relieved when I saw the marching dots indicating she was writing another message.

Want some company?

More than anything.

32

Flynn

When I drove up to the cabin and saw Paxon sitting on the porch swing, I smiled. I'd hoped that was where he'd be.

I parked, and he stood and waited while I grabbed something from the passenger seat.

"What's this?" he asked when I handed him the bag.

"Dessert."

"Wow. You're spoiling me."

"Someone should."

With those words, his eyes met mine. "Thank you, Flynn. It's been a long time since..."

"Since what?"

"I don't want to make it sound like Cope, Decker, and the other guys on my detail haven't taken care of me. Each one has risked their life for mine." He held up the bag. "This is...different."

"I can promise you I did not risk my life making peach cobbler." I smiled, and so did he.

"It means a lot."

"Wanna share it?" I asked, knowing I'd brought plenty for two.

"I'd love that."

I stopped him when he went to go inside. "Everything we need is in that bag."

He pulled out two napkins, forks, spoons, and the cobbler. "It's still warm."

"Which means the ice cream on top is probably melted."

He opened the lid and breathed in. "It smells so good."

"Let's hope it tastes good too."

We sat on the swing and dug in with our spoons.

"I ate almost all of it," Paxon said, pointing to the two or three bites that were left.

"I only wanted a taste anyway."

"Now I feel bad."

I laughed and stood when he did. "Don't waste the energy." I'm not sure what possessed me to do it, but I put my hand on his arm, reached up, and kissed his cheek.

The reaction I got couldn't have been worse.

33

Irish

My only explanation was that Flynn had caught me off guard. When she kissed my cheek, instead of kissing her back or even smiling, I took an abrupt step backwards.

"Sorry," she mumbled as she ran down the porch steps and over to her truck. She was inside, with the engine started, before I came out of my stupor enough to go after her. By then, it was too late.

When Cope texted me the next day, shortly after daylight, asking if I was ready to get to work, I told him I wanted to be on my own this morning. When Decker knocked on the door shortly thereafter, I told him to go the fuck away.

"Open up, Irish. You know if you don't, I'll come in anyway."

"Do you have no respect for personal space?" I asked, flinging the door open.

"None whatsoever." Instead of coming inside, he stood on the porch. "We're going to work at the other cabin this morning. That way, Ali won't be on her own all day."

"Go right ahead. I can get just as much done from here."

"Knock it off. Whatever happened, get over it, and get your ass next door."

I didn't remember much about my father. I wasn't even in double digits when he died, but the tone of Decker's voice sent me straight back to being a little kid. Instead of arguing with him, I grabbed my laptop and followed him next door. It didn't dawn on me until we were walking that he'd realized "something" had, in fact, happened. That made me feel more like a child.

Ali opened the door, and instead of stepping aside so we could both come in, she only let Decker pass.

"You need a hug." She stepped closer and embraced me.

"Yeah? How can you tell?"

She let go and cocked her head. "Honestly, Irish, I think you need one every time I see you."

I put my hands on her shoulders. "How are you feeling?"

"Morning sickness sucks donkey balls." She rubbed her stomach. "But it's so worth it."

"I don't really know what questions to ask."

Ali laughed. "I'm about eight weeks along. We weren't trying, but we weren't not trying, if that makes sense."

Being of Irish descent, my skin was pale, which meant I flushed easily, as I was now.

"I'll stop embarrassing you. Cope has been digging into this Xander thing since last night." She motioned to where he sat at the table, head propped on his hand.

"Did he sleep?"

"Not that I know of."

"Hey," I said, walking over and squeezing his shoulder. "Find anything?"

"Probably nothing more than you did. Here's what I don't get. What's with 'Xander'? His middle name is Clark. William Clark Harris."

I hadn't given it any thought, but as soon as Cope said it, I had a guess. "Alexander the Great."

Decker raised his head. "The defender of the Argead."

"Or it isn't related at all," Cope grumbled.

"It is. I'm sure of it," said Decker. "There wasn't time for a briefing, but I…uh…have a recording of Stella and Kerr's conversation."

It was Decker's hesitation that made me raise my head. "She was wired?"

More than his hesitation, the flush of his cheeks told me that Stella hadn't been aware she was. Now wasn't the time for me to get high and mighty about it. In fact, there'd never be a time for me to question Decker's means or motives. I trusted him, and he'd kept me alive. Not just me, countless other agents. I would never doubt his intentions were for the greater good of just that—the good. Like everyone I'd worked with on the Invincibles team, I believed their agenda was the same as mine: to rid the world of as much of the evil we could as long as we walked the face of it.

What we heard was similar to what Burns had told us about Nicholas Kerr, except Stella's conversation with him made chills run up and down my spine.

"Tiffany Joy, at last we meet."

There was silence as if he was waiting for a response.

"So much like your aunt. You're weak like she was. Your only power is in your pen. Otherwise, you are mute."

"You didn't know her very well, and you don't know me at all."

"Ah, she does have a voice, but where is the reporter, eh? Are you too afraid I'll kill you to ask me any questions?"

"You're going to kill me whether I ask or not, just like you did Barb and Nancy."

"Yes, well, that is probably true."

"Does your wife know you killed her aunt like you did mine?"

"She knows I had no choice."

Stella continued to prod him. It was evident in the change in the tone of his voice that Kerr was getting angry.

"Your aunt believed she could take on the world, that once she exposed the corruption she thought she'd found, that would be the end of it. What she—and you—and people like Veronica Guerin failed to recognize was that it is the very corruption they railed against that keeps the world spinning. Bribes, power plays, deals negotiated in back alleys, that is how it really works. You see world leaders on television, shaking hands as they sign agreements, flashbulbs going off around them—all of that is for show. The real deals were made months, even years, before the stage is set for the public to see. In that time, those who threaten to tear down the carefully mastered plans of men like me, are eliminated."

"Eliminated? As in agents around the world being assassinated?" Stella asked.

"You are so sure they were the good and I am evil. Your naivete is so common, so typical. Without men like me, you would be nothing."

"Because I'm a woman?"

"Because you're a stupid woman."

God, it was amazing she didn't pull out her gun and shoot him right then. I would've.

"You say that men like you are the real deal makers. Is that how you justify lining your pockets with millions of dollars? You say that all you do is for the greater good, but when your day of reckoning comes, you know as well as I do that you were nothing but a thief. A common criminal. A murderer who only ever knew how to steal, never how to earn your way in the world."

"So like her," he mumbled. I assumed he was talking about Stella's aunt. His next words confirmed it.

"What Barb found was merely the tip of the iceberg. As if anyone in the world truly cares what goes on at Interpol. It serves merely as a clearinghouse for those of us in the intelligence business to burn evidence before it lands in the hands of someone like your aunt. Or you."

"Are you saying Operation Argead goes beyond Interpol?"

Kerr's laughter at Stella's question could only be described as maniacal. "I'm saying that without the voluntary contributions that come through Interpol and countless other organizations like it, the intelligence community, even entire governments, would crumble with lack of funding. No, little girl, our reach is global. Even the most powerful countries—the United States, Russia, China—all rely on Argead. Without us, they would be nothing."

"Sounds like you've let a little power go to your head. You can't really believe that you and your little group of intelligence has-beens truly affect world governments."

"As I anticipated, this is all too much for your small mind to comprehend. I've grown weary of your tedium. Hand over the evidence now so I don't have to dirty my hands with your blood in order to retrieve it."

We heard the sound of guns being fired in the background and then Stella say, "You know what? Fuck it," followed by a close-range shot.

Decker hit a button on his laptop. "The rest is the team coming in, along with the aftermath, none of which provides information we don't already have."

Cope stood. "I don't know about the rest of you, but I need a drink." He looked over at Ali. "Sorry, baby."

"It's okay," she said, smiling. "I'll get it. How many glasses?"

When Decker and I both nodded and thanked her, she brought a bottle and three glasses from the kitchen and set them on the table.

"I don't know whether to have a shot because I need one after listening to Kerr's diatribe or to toast the fact that we might, truly, be getting to the end of this," said Cope.

"Both," I responded.

Ali poured two fingers in each glass, and we downed it without a word. She refilled them, and Decker stood.

"I vote for three because I have to insert a toast of my own."

We raised our glasses to his.

"Here's to the two of you. Without your bravery, tenacity, resourcefulness, selflessness—I could go on and on—Kerr and everyone who came before or after, would continue." He looked directly at me. "Irish, you have given your all more than anyone in this room. I only hope that someday everyone in the world will know what a true hero and patriot you are."

I couldn't fight the tears his words moved me to. Even after enduring so much hatred, it wasn't easy to accept his praise.

"Thank you," I said when my emotion eased enough for me to speak.

"Buck and Stella are in the air now," said Decker, looking at his phone. "Our esteemed visitors should be arriving within a couple of hours as well. If you need some time, you'd be wise to take it now."

I wasn't sure if Decker was speaking to Cope and Ali or to me. Either way, that was my cue to head out.

"We'll meet at fourteen hundred hours," he added when I stood and picked up my laptop. "At the main house."

"Roger that."

The way Flynn left the other day had been weighing heavily on my mind and not because of anything she did. It was all me. She'd given me an innocent kiss on the cheek, and I'd behaved like it was a snake bite.

I was getting damn tired of not having a way to get around the ranch on my own. "What's somebody gotta do to have access to a vehicle?"

"Here," said Cope, tossing me a set of keys.

"Where are you off to?" asked Decker.

"You still my fucking nursemaid?"

Decker laughed. "No, I wanted a ride, asshole. But in the mood you're in, I'd rather walk."

"I'm going to the dining hall. Either get in the truck now, or figure it out on your own."

"That's what I like to see," he said, walking past me and squeezing my shoulder. "Irish takin' charge."

When I pulled up, Decker walked in the direction of the main house and I went the opposite way.

"Can I help you?" a man who looked vaguely familiar asked.

"I'm looking for Flynn."

"She's not in today."

"I see."

"Can I tell her who stopped by?"

"Paxon."

34

Flynn

I waited until I was sure Paxon was gone before I came into the kitchen from the storage room where I'd gone to hide when I saw him drive up.

"Thanks, Paco."

"Man, Flynn, don't ask me to lie for you again. That guy looked like someone kicked his damn puppy." Paco rubbed his chest and winked.

"I'm sorry. I just didn't want to talk to him right now." I felt my eyes fill with tears like they did every time I thought about Paxon's reaction to me attempting to kiss his cheek. I'd suffered through a lot of humiliation in my short life, but that had to have been the worst. It was like I was a six-year-old and giving him cooties.

"Come here," said Paco, motioning to the chair he'd pulled away from the table. When I sat, he did too.

"I've seen you with him. What's his name? Paxon?"

"Everyone calls him Irish."

"That's a weird name too but better than Paxon," he mumbled and then looked into my eyes. "He seems like a decent guy. Tell ol' Paco what happened."

I laughed. "Ol' Paco? What are you, twenty-five?"

"Older than you. Now, quit changing the subject. What happened?"

"It was nothing."

"Right. That's why you hid in the storeroom."

Both Paco and I raised our heads when we heard the dining hall door open again. Paxon walked in, holding up a piece of paper. If I could crawl into a hole and disappear, I would. Now I felt even worse about asking Paco to lie.

"I was going to leave a note." Paxon's cheeks were flushed. I was upset with him for humiliating me, but I'd just done the same thing to him.

Paco got up and left the room. Paxon walked over and took his seat.

"I'd avoid me too if I were you," he said.

I looked everywhere but at him. "What I did was inappropriate, and I'm sorry."

"I don't accept your apology."

I met his gaze. "Why not?"

"Because you did nothing wrong."

"You acted like—"

"A jackass."

I shook my head.

He reached over and put his hand on mine. "I really like you, Flynn. In fact, I worry that I might like you too much."

"You don't have to do this."

"Be honest with you?"

"Explain anything. You already said you wanted us to be friends. I'm the one who crossed the line."

"Kissing someone on the cheek isn't crossing the line." He took a deep breath and let it out slowly. "I think I told you that I haven't exactly lived a normal life the last few years. That includes not having a lot of human contact."

I wanted to say I'd never had human contact, but stopped myself. I already felt pathetic enough without him needing to know I'd never even been kissed by a man.

He looked outside when two black SUVs drove by.

"Who is that?" I asked.

"Hard to say. There are a lot of people arriving today."

"Because of your mission?"

"That's right. We believe we've stumbled on two promising leads. We'll be breaking into teams so we can follow up on both simultaneously."

"I hope it goes well."

He let out another breath I hadn't realized he was holding. "Me too."

"You should probably go," I said when I saw three more SUVs drive by.

"I probably should, but first, I want to tell you that I won't have a lot of free time in the next few days. Maybe longer. But when I do, I'd like to get together and talk some more."

I pushed my chair back and stood. "That won't be necessary."

"Flynn?" he called after me, but I kept walking.

35

Irish

By the time I got to the main house, there was a crowd of people inside and more SUVs arriving. As I walked by people I'd heard of more than knew, several heads nodded in my direction.

"Irish," said Razor Sharp, stepping away from two others I recognized. "Do you know Gunner Godet?"

"Not until now."

Gunner joined us and shook my hand. "Shoulda called in K19 a long time ago, Irish. We woulda backed ya."

"Hey, now," said Doc. "Let's not start with that shit. We're backing him now. That's what matters." Doc shook my hand like Gunner had.

As I made my way to the front of the room, my eyes met Decker's, and he motioned to where he wanted me to sit.

"I heard from Buck. He, Stella, and the rest of the crew should be here in fifteen."

I stood when Burns Butler approached.

"Sit down, please," he said, taking the chair beside me. When he didn't speak, I surveyed the room from a new angle. There were men here I'd read about most of my career and doubted I'd ever meet, let alone work with.

"You ready for this?" asked Decker, approaching with Doc.

"I'm not sure having me in charge of this mission is such a good idea. There are others here—"

Burns slowly turned his head, but it was his hand on my arm that made me stop talking. "There is no one better."

My eyes met Rile DeLéon's, who was seated next to Kensington Whitby, his soon-to-be wife, from what I'd heard. I didn't see Grinder, but Decker had mentioned he was in Italy and his wife was due to have a baby at any moment. She wasn't the only one. I'd heard Decker's wife was too. I didn't see Edge either.

The door opened, and Buck walked in with Stella, who looked as much like a deer in headlights as I probably did. I raised a hand, and she waved back.

Moments later, Ali came through the same door followed by Cope and Money McTiernan. No one had mentioned he would be attending this meeting. I wondered if Cope's father would be.

Decker stepped to the front of the room, and Doc joined him. I was about to turn around to face them when someone else caught my eye.

"Did you know they were coming?" I asked Deck, motioning with my head to where Lynx and Emme stood just inside the door.

"Affirmative," he responded, raising a brow. "But I wasn't aware he was."

I shifted my body so I could see through what was becoming a crowd. "What the fuck?" I said under my breath when I saw Niven "Saint" St. Thomas walk up and stand beside Lynx.

I turned toward Decker, who shrugged.

"If we could have everyone's attention, please," he said a few minutes later. "It might be easier if you all took a seat."

Decker and Doc remained standing when everyone else sat. "In the absence of two, I'm going to speak on behalf of the four founding partners of the Invincible Intelligence and Security Group," said Decker, looking at Rile.

"And in the absence of one, I'll speak on behalf of the four founding partners of K19 Security Solutions," said Doc, nodding at Razor and Gunner.

"What's with all the formality?" Razor said loud enough for everyone to hear. "We aren't getting married, are we?"

"We're already married," answered Gunner.

"No," said Doc. "We aren't getting married. However, we are about to take on our first joint mission. IISG and K19 have been contracted by the CIA, backed by the full support of the Senate Intelligence Committee, to proceed full throttle in a mission designed to wipe every last person affiliated with Operation Argead from the face of the earth."

"I'm not sure that was the exact directive, Doc," called out Money.

"You say tomato, I say annihilation," Doc responded. "Same difference."

"Irish Warrick will serve as lead," said Deck, motioning for me to join them.

I waited, stunned when the room erupted in applause.

"Irish," said Decker, stepping to the side like Doc had and giving me my cue to proceed the way we'd talked about.

"We'll begin at zero eight hundred tomorrow, if that's okay with Stella."

"Um. Sure," she said, shrugging. I motioned for her to join us at the front of the room.

"For the next three days, we'll review all the leads we have so far, including those which came out in the most recent intelligence bulletin." I heard several people muttering and waited until they quieted down. I turned to Stella. "Whenever you're ready, we'll also review whatever evidence Barb left that you brought back from New York. Okay by you?" I asked.

"Sounds great," she responded but only loud enough for those of us close to her to hear.

"Stella, if she agrees, will serve as my second-in-command," I announced, pausing while everyone in the room clapped a second time.

I leaned closer. "Well? Will you?"

"Yes, Irish. I would be honored."

"Everyone heard that, right?" I waited for the laughter to die down. "Unless there are any questions, we'll convene back here tomorrow."

A hand went up in the rear of the room.

"Yes, Buck?" I asked. "You have questions?"

"Just one."

"Go ahead."

He stood. "I was just wondering who Stella works for. IISG or K19?"

"She works for us," both Decker and Doc answered. There was more laughter, followed by people standing and walking up to those they hadn't yet greeted.

I stayed where I was, wishing there was another door I could leave through.

"Paxon?" I heard a familiar voice say and turned to look into Emme's eyes. I didn't have a chance to respond before she threw her arms around me.

"I'm so sorry I ever doubted you." It sounded as though she was crying.

I pulled back so I could look into her eyes. "You were set up to doubt me. Everything went according to the plan."

"Irish," said Lynx, walking up behind Emme.

"I was just apologizing," she explained. Lynx put his arm around her shoulders.

"As I already said, there's nothing to apologize for."

"I feel as though I should as well," said Lynx. "I was probably the biggest wanker of all."

While I laughed, it certainly wasn't authentic, especially when Saint joined us.

"Irish," he said.

"Saint." When the door opened again and I saw Flynn walk in, I quickly excused myself.

"Hey," I said, rushing over to her.

"Hey, um, I'm supposed to let you know dinner is ready whenever your meeting is over."

I waved my hand in the direction of the crowd of people. "As you can see, it's over."

"Would you mind?"

"Not at all." I whistled. "Can I have everyone's attention? Dinner is being served at the dining hall for anyone who's hungry." I was about to turn and follow Flynn out when my eyes landed on Saint. What I saw, I didn't like. He was laser-focused on Flynn and heading our way.

"I'll walk over with you," I offered.

"You seem…busy."

"Not at all." I put my hand on the small of Flynn's back and followed her outside. "Thank you for making dinner for everyone."

"It's what I do, Paxon," she said, smiling for the first time that I'd seen today.

"It's a lot more people."

She shrugged. "Recipes are easy to double."

"What are you serving?"

"Cord smoked brisket and sausage and barbecued chicken breasts."

"Are you serving your potato salad?"

"Yes. Baked beans and coleslaw too."

"It sounds really good, Flynn." I cleared my throat and stopped walking. "I know I said things were going to be hectic, but our first real meeting isn't until tomorrow. I was wondering if you would consider stopping by later?"

Unlike me, she hadn't stopped walking. "I don't think that's a good idea, Paxon," she said before going inside.

"Pretty girl," said Saint, walking up behind me. "Who is she?"

"Buck's sister. Leave her alone."

Saint smirked. "As you are?"

I didn't laugh. "I mean it, Saint."

He chuckled all the way inside the same building Flynn had gone into.

Two hours later, everyone was still in the dining hall, sitting around and shooting the shit. I asked Buck if we should head out so their crew could clean up, but he said it wasn't necessary.

A few minutes later, Holt walked in carrying a guitar. He wasn't alone, either. Ben Rice was with him. I hadn't noticed the two stools and mics set up near the back of the room until they walked over and set their guitar cases on the floor.

Buck introduced them to the crowd while people from the kitchen came out and moved tables and chairs away so there'd be room to dance. Flynn, though, was nowhere to be seen.

Three or four songs in, people began dancing even though there were very few women in attendance. I kept a nervous eye out for Flynn, hoping that if she did come out of the kitchen, I could get to her before Saint did.

"You okay?" asked Decker, coming to stand beside me.

"Why is Saint here?"

"Good question. A better question would be why neither of us was informed he would be."

"Did Doc know he was coming?"

"Negative."

"He came with Lynx and Dr. Charles."

"Dr. Edgemon now."

"Whatever."

"Dr. Benjamin's involvement in this is still a mystery. Perhaps one Saint can solve."

I scoffed. "I'd like this mission to end before I'm ninety. If we're looking for help from Saint, I might not live to see it."

Several things happened simultaneously. The door to the dining hall opened, and Flynn walked inside. As if

HEATHER SLADE

he were a bird of prey sweeping in to devour his dinner, Saint was by her side in mere seconds. I watched in near agony as he led her out to the dance floor.

"I'd cut in quick if I were you."

"I don't think Flynn would appreciate my doing so."

Decker shrugged and walked away.

I had every intention of doing as he'd suggested, just not right away. Waiting, though, made it more difficult. When one song ended and another began, someone else cut in before I had a chance.

Most didn't bother me. It was only Saint's gaze, that never seemed to leave her, that made me angrier by the minute. Flynn was an innocent young woman who he would devastate if he came at her in the way he was known to do. At the very minimum, I had to warn her.

I stalked over and tapped her current dance partner, Razor, on the shoulder. When he took a gentlemanly step back, I pulled Flynn into my arms. Her cheeks were flushed, and she was smiling.

"You're having a good time," I said, shuffling my feet from side to side and wishing I was a better dancer.

"To be honest, my feet are starting to hurt," she said, laughing. "I haven't had a chance to break these boots in."

256

IRISHED

I looked down at the cowboy boots I remembered her wearing the night we went to the Flying R. The first night I held her in my arms.

"You look very pretty, Flynn."

She looked away. "Thank you."

"I...um...wanted to warn you about one of the guys here tonight. He's got a reputation as—"

"Oh my God." Flynn wriggled from my arms and stalked away, but I stayed on her heels.

"Wait. Please." Given I was taller, had a longer stride, and wasn't wearing boots that hurt my feet, it was easy for me to get in front of her before she stormed out the door.

"Paxon, you better just get out of my way."

"Only if you'll let me finish."

36

Flynn

"Why? Why should I let you finish? Don't you real-ize...never mind. You couldn't possibly understand."

"Understand what?"

I stomped away, but Irish followed. I was almost to the front door of the main house when he grabbed my arm.

"Understand what?" he repeated.

I knew I'd soon be in tears, but what I was about to say needed to be said. "I thought maybe—just maybe—this would be the year I'd finally have a man interested in me. You said I was pretty. You danced with me, held me in your arms." My eyes filled with tears, and my voice was too clogged with emotion to go on.

He turned my body so my back was up against the porch rail. "I am interested in you, Flynn. I told you that."

I rolled my eyes and wiped my tears with my sleeve. "Right. So interested in me that when I kissed you, you couldn't move away fast enough."

He cupped my cheek with his hand. "I'm sorry, sweetheart. I know it doesn't make a lot of sense, but I explained that too."

"I just—" I started crying again, unable to go on.

"Just what?" He stroked my skin with his thumb and rested his forehead against mine.

"I just wanted to know how it felt to be kissed by a man. You wouldn't do it, and now you're warning me about other guys—"

When Paxon's lips touched mine, my mind went blank. He held the side of my face and pressed his tongue against my mouth, and I opened to him.

His kiss was soft at first, then harder when he angled his head. His other arm went around my waist, and he pulled my body into his.

Paxon stared into my eyes. "I've wanted to do that since I met you. I should have. I'm sorry I waited."

Before I could respond, he kissed me again, and it was heavenly. His lips were soft, but the tip of his tongue was hard as it went deeper into my mouth. I pressed my body against his, and the vibration of his moan traveled from his chest into mine. When I tried to back away, he held me tighter.

I got lost in the feel of his mouth on mine, so when he stopped abruptly, it threw me.

"What?" I asked, noticing he was looking over my shoulder. I turned my head and saw someone watching us. "Is that who you were warning me about?"

"Yes," he said, shifting us over.

"I'd invite you inside, but my brothers…"

Paxon studied me.

"What?"

"I don't want to say good night, but I don't want to return to the dining hall either."

"We could go to your cabin."

"Would you be comfortable going there?"

For a second, I thought he was joking, but the look on his face hadn't changed.

"Why wouldn't I be?"

"Being there alone with me?"

"I've been there alone with you before, Paxon." I reached into my pocket, pulled out the key to my truck, and put it in his palm. "Let's go."

I kept my head down as we walked from the porch to my vehicle, so I didn't know if the man was watching any longer or not. When Paxon opened the passenger door but kissed me again before I could climb inside, I guessed he probably wasn't.

"Come over here," he said once he got in the driver's side. I scooted to the middle, loving that my old truck didn't have bucket seats. Paxon draped his right arm across my lap and pulled me even closer. Before putting the truck in gear, he kissed me again. He pulled back. "Am I making you uncomfortable?"

"That's the second time you've asked me a similar question. Why do you think you would be?"

He kissed me again. "Because now that I've started, I don't want to stop."

"I don't want to stop either."

"Flynn…"

"Whatever you have to say, we can talk about when we get to your cabin."

He put the truck in gear and drove away from the dining hall.

When we got to the cabin, he cut the engine but didn't open his door.

"Is everything okay?" I asked.

"I think so."

"Why aren't you getting out of the truck?"

"I want you to know that I meant what I said earlier. I've wanted to kiss you since the moment I met you. I know it sounds like a line, but I felt an immediate connection."

"I felt it too."

Paxon turned to face me. "You did?"

I nodded. "Can we go inside now?"

He laughed. "Sure." He opened the door, climbed out, and held out his hand. When I jumped down, he put a hand on either side of me and kissed me one more time before leading me inside.

37

Irish

It had been a long time since I'd been with a woman, not that I had any intention of being with Flynn tonight. However, things had changed between us, and I needed to be mindful of what I now knew was her complete innocence.

"Can I get you anything?" I asked.

"Water would be nice." She rubbed her arms.

"Are you cold?"

"A little chilly. I can start a fire if you'd like."

I thought about telling her I'd do it, but she'd probably been the one who put the logs in the fireplace to begin with.

When I brought her water over, I saw she'd propped some of the pillows from the sofa onto the floor. I sat down beside her and watched the fire spread from the kindling to the logs.

"Of all the cabins on the ranch, this has always been my favorite."

"Yeah? How come?"

She shrugged. "I can't really say. It's just got a nice feel to it."

I put my arm around her and snuggled her close to me. "I've had a condo in DC for several years. I haven't spent much time there for the last couple, but even before that, it never felt as warm and inviting as this place. Probably because you've made it feel that way."

I loved the way her cheeks turned pink whenever I complimented her.

"Flynn, I need to tell you—"

"Paxon, I swear to God, if you're about to tell me we can only be friends again—"

I cut her off with another kiss and then rested my forehead against hers. "No, sweetheart. That wasn't what I was going to say."

"Anything remotely close to that?"

I shook my head.

"Okay, go ahead and say whatever it is."

"I told you earlier that things were going to be hectic for the next few days. As much as I know I'll want to spend time with you, I may not have much of it to spare."

"You don't have to explain. I understand." She rested her head on my shoulder and sighed.

"I feel like there's something else you want to say."

"There's a lot, actually."

I slid down so I was lying on the floor rather than sitting up, rested my head on the pillow, and brought Flynn with me. I kept my arm around her, and she turned and put her arm around my waist.

"I'm ready to hear whatever you have to say, Flynn."

She took a deep breath. "I unloaded a lot of stuff on you earlier. I hope you aren't feeling sorry for me."

I turned to face her. "I'm not. I promise."

"I'm sure you know my story already since it's Buck's story too, but my mother died when I was three years old."

"I did know that."

"My father never remarried, so I grew up with four brothers and a dad who didn't seem to care whether I had a female role model. I wasn't lying when I said I never wore dresses. The one I had on at the Flying R was the first one I ever owned."

"Is this the second?" I asked, running my fingers across its bodice.

When Flynn shuddered, I moved my hand away. She put it back, and I smiled. "It's the third. Actually, it's one of many."

"Each one prettier than the one before it." This time, instead of running my finger over the fabric, I touched her skin where the two met. Flynn leaned forward, and I kissed her, pulling her so her body rested on mine.

"I'm too heavy," she said, attempting to move away, but I wouldn't let her.

"You're perfect."

She lowered her gaze. "I'm the furthest thing from it."

I put my finger on her chin and raised her face so I could see her eyes. "You're perfect," I repeated. "Every part of you is. Not just your beautiful face." I touched her lips with my finger. "Or your body that makes me want to hold it next to me whenever I'm with you." I trailed my fingers along her dress like I had a minute ago and then rested my hand just below her shoulder. "This is the most beautiful part of all. I knew as soon as I met you that you had a kind heart."

"I felt the same about you."

"Sometimes, I wonder if there's anything left of mine."

She put her hand on my left pec. "It's whole, Paxon."

"How can you be so sure?"

"Same way you're sure mine is kind." She rested her head on my chest. "Tell me about your life before this mission."

It was hard to remember there was a "before," and I said so. "My life before I joined the CIA was pretty dull. My dad died when I was eight. My mom died not long after I graduated from college. No brothers or sisters, not even cousins."

"Did you have a lot of friends in school?"

"Nah. I was more of a loner."

"Like me, although probably for a different reason."

"I've never been much of a talker. People probably figured I was an asshole, so they didn't bother trying to get to know me."

"Seems like you have a lot of friends now."

"Friends? I don't know about that. Work colleagues."

"What about Cope?"

I laughed. "I guess he's my friend. Although, when I first met him, I couldn't stand him."

"Tell me why."

We talked until well past midnight, only stopping every so often to get lost in more kisses. Every time she said she should go, I held her tight, not wanting her to leave. Finally, we both fell asleep.

When I woke, the sun was coming up. Flynn's back was to my front, and I had my arm around her waist. When I moved it, her eyes opened and she stretched.

"What time is it?" she asked.

"Almost six."

I expected her to say she had to rush off, but she smiled up at me.

"Do you know how much I wish I could spend the whole day with you? Tonight too?"

"As much as I'd like to spend it with you, Paxon."

I held out my hand, she took it, and I pulled her to her feet. "I can't believe I'm saying this, but are you supposed to be at the dining hall?"

She smiled and wrapped her arms around my waist. "Today is my day off."

I put my arms around her and groaned. "Now I really wish I could take the day off too."

She leaned up and kissed me. "It's okay. I have plans this morning anyway."

"Yeah?"

"I'm having breakfast with two friends in Gunnison."

I loved how pleased she sounded. "Who are they?"

That question made her cheeks turn pink. "Nina and Lucy. They're the ones who helped me pick out new clothes and fix my hair."

I brushed the wisps from her face, kissed each of her eyelids, the tip of her nose, and her lips. I stopped myself from continuing down the side of her neck, knowing then I'd be starting something neither of us was ready for.

"Do you think you'll be working all night?" she asked.

"I hope not, but it depends on how much we're able to accomplish today."

"If you happen to quit early, maybe I could come over."

"I would love it. How late is early?"

She laughed. "Text me when you're finishing up, and if I'm still awake, that'll be early."

When Flynn left, I climbed into the coldest shower I could stand. When I got out and looked in the mirror, I hardly recognized the man staring back at me. I'd so rarely seen him smile.

"You're in a good mood this morning," said Ali, nudging me with her arm when I came out of the cabin and saw her and Cope waiting for me.

"You can tell that just by looking at my face?"

"Yep," answered Cope. "Not to mention that when we got up, she looked out the window and saw Buck's sister doing the walk of shame right after sunrise."

The smile left my face. "It wasn't like that."

"Settle down, Irish. I was just joking. Although, we did see her truck last night when we returned from the dining hall, so I don't think you can get away with telling us she came by to drop something off this morning."

"She stayed over, okay? But nothing happened."

Ali put her arm through mine as we walked to the waiting SUV. "Either way, Irish. It's none of our business. I'm just happy to see you happy."

Five minutes after we walked into the ranch house where we were scheduled to meet, every bit of happiness I'd felt was knocked out of me when I saw someone I'd expected even less than Saint.

"What the fuck is Dr. Benjamin doing here?" I barked at Decker, whose head snapped up.

"It was in the brief I sent this morning."

"I didn't have a chance to read it."

He raised a brow.

"I'll do it now." I sat at a table and opened my laptop. When I got done reading, I wasn't any happier about Benjamin's arrival than I had been when I saw him. It had been Saint who suggested he join us, and from what I read, the only person he'd cleared it with was Lynx.

"I thought I was the lead on this part of the investigation."

"You are."

"Then why wasn't I read in on it before it happened?"

"That's a question you're going to have to ask for yourself." Decker motioned with his head to where Lynx and Emme were standing. I stalked over to them.

"A word," I said to Lynx, also motioning to Saint. They both followed me out the door to the front porch.

I spun around on them. "I don't know what chain of command the two of you believe you're operating under, but for this mission, I'm at the top. Everything that happens with it from here until it's called, goes through me. In my absence, it goes through Stella. Are we clear?"

"What's this about?" asked Lynx.

"Dr. Benjamin."

"What of him? The man is an MI6 asset."

"I don't care if he's the chief of MI6. You should've cleared it with me before bringing him here."

An SUV pulled up, and Doc Butler got out along with Razor Sharp and Gunner Godet. "Good morning, gentlemen," said Doc, walking up to join us. The other two men went inside. "Anything you want to read me in on."

"Irish was just informing us we should've cleared Benjamin's arrival through him," said Saint.

Doc turned to me. "That's my fault. They cleared it with me. I apologize, Irish."

I was livid but nodded. "Is there anyone else you cleared?"

The man looked contrite, which made me feel like an asshole.

"Negative." He turned to the other two men. "Lynx, Saint, would you please excuse us?"

They went inside, leaving me alone with Doc.

"Look, I'm sorry I snapped about Benjamin. The truth is, I hadn't expected the two of them, either."

"Understood. Is there a problem you need to make me aware of?"

"Negative."

"Irish, are you sure?"

I had nothing to go on but my gut, and it could very well be that my reaction to Lynx, Saint, and Dr. Benjamin was a direct result of the part of the op that took place in Cambridge. Even my thinking Benjamin was one of the men I thought I saw in Hong Kong nine years ago could've been clouded by my experience with Lynx and Emme as well as the prejudice I'd felt against Saint since I'd first heard he was the agent being sent in by MI6.

"I'm sure."

"If that changes, let me know."

I followed Doc inside. Before I could get much past the entrance, Cope intercepted me. "What is Dr. Benjamin doing here?" he asked.

"I asked the same thing. Apparently, Lynx ran it past Doc, who approved him joining us."

"Why?"

Before I could respond, Decker joined us and motioned back outside.

"According to Doc, Saint believes Dr. Benjamin may be able to assist with our investigation—enough that it warranted bringing him here."

"Why didn't either of them say that?" I didn't expect an answer to my rhetorical question and didn't get one.

"What do you want to do?" Decker asked.

"For now, he stays. If at any time I believe he shouldn't, he's gone. Same with Saint."

"Roger that," said Decker.

"Tell him about Hong Kong," said Cope, nudging me.

"That first mission, the one when Dingo, 337, and Julius were taken out. I saw two men right before the hit was carried out. It was from a distance, but I believe Dr. Benjamin was one of those men."

Decker nodded his head slowly. "In that case, perhaps the doctor is exactly where we want him."

38

Irish

We broke into four teams, each with a task list.

Stella, Buck, and Rile focused on sorting through the stockpile of evidence her aunt had left her in a vault, in Tiffany's no less.

Burns, Doc, Gunner, and Razor centered their attention on Ming Shen-Lin and Nicholas Kerr along with Stanley Donofrio and Antoine Moreau, the two men who'd served on Interpol's executive committee years ago when Kerr was president. Up until two days ago, Kerr had been the sole survivor of the four.

Decker led a team made up of Lynx, Emme, Saint, and Dr. Benjamin. Their area of concentration was the current executive committee—Daniel Byrne, also recently deceased, Boris Antonov, and Chen Wang-Su aka Kim Ha-joon.

My team—including Cope, Ali, and Money—concentrated our efforts on the man the Chinese government had recently granted permanent asylum, William "Xander" Harris.

With the evidence Money was able to gather, we had a clear picture of the level and amount of intelligence he'd systematically released over the course of ten years. Just in sheer documentation, it numbered in the tens of thousands.

Figuring out his motive wasn't difficult. The boy who'd watched his father go off to two wars grew into a man whose father committed suicide outside a VA hospital after allegedly being denied treatment for a combination of Gulf War Syndrome and PTSD.

That suicide took place one year before I first met Sumner Copeland at The Farm.

Like with the deaths of the agents I'd been tracking, I sat back in my chair, closed my eyes, and offered a moment of reverent silence for the man, the soldier, the patriot—Herbert Harris. He'd proudly served his country, not once but twice, and his country let him down in his time of need. When tears leaked from the corners of my eyes, I didn't try to hide them. Mr. Harris' death was a tragedy like every other we were investigating.

Ali reached over and put her hand on my arm. "Irish, are you okay?"

I shook my head. "I just need a minute." When I opened my eyes, the first thing I saw was Flynn walking from the dining hall to another entrance that led into the main house. "Excuse me."

I pushed back my chair, stood, and went outside, hoping I'd catch her.

"Hey, Paxon," she said, turning to look when I approached.

"Hi, Flynn. How was breakfast?"

She studied me. "It was nice. Rough morning?"

I nodded, unable to speak. When I reached for her, she wrapped her arms around my waist and gave me the hug I so desperately needed—not just today, but hundreds of times over the course of the last few years. She held me so tight, as though she knew exactly how to comfort me, even without knowing why I needed it. I lost track of how long we embraced, outside where it could be witnessed by everyone meeting in the main room of the house as well as anyone going in and out of the barn or dining hall. When I looked into her eyes, she didn't seem embarrassed or uncomfortable as I feared she might.

"Thank you." I leaned forward and brushed her lips with mine.

"Anytime, Paxon. It brings me as much comfort as it does you."

I rested my forehead against hers. "So wise beyond your years."

"I don't know if it's wisdom or instinct."

"Both." I kissed her one more time. "I hate to say this, but I should get back in there."

"If you need another one of those, you have my number."

"Yeah, if I call, you'll come just to give me a hug?"

"Every time."

No one looked up when I came inside, not even Ali. When I pulled my chair out and sat beside her, she glanced in my direction.

"I really like her," she whispered.

"So do I."

"Hey, Irish," I heard Razor say from across the room. "Can you come take a look at this?"

I bent over his laptop, looking at a blurry image of two people. Beside it, was a gravestone. I read the inscription indicating the deceased had only lived to be twenty-five years old. "Stephen Kerr?"

"Nicholas Kerr's only son," answered Burns.

"According to what Razor found, he was killed in action during the Gulf War," said Gunner, turning to Doc.

"I reached out to Z Alexander, who located a brief indicating that his death was reported as friendly fire."

I pulled out a chair and sat down to take in what I'd just heard.

"There was a witness," Doc added. "Army Sergeant H.J. Harris."

"Herbert Harris? Xander's father?" I asked.

"It would appear so."

"Any other connection you can find between Kerr and either the father or the son?"

"I had a buddy of mine run through what would now be considered ancient records, given they're on microfiche, but we hit pay dirt," said Razor. "Kerr traveled from the UK to the States the day of Harris' funeral. He stayed in Maryland, where it was held, for two days before returning to London."

"Tell him what else you found," said Gunner, slugging Razor's arm.

"Enigma Computers, who Xander went to work for after leaving the CIA, is 'owned' by a shell corporation—no big surprise there. However, I was able to 'trace' the money trail back to a holding company headquartered in Hong Kong."

There was no doubt in my mind that the emphasis he placed on the word traced in reality meant hacked. "And?"

"Both Nicholas Kerr and Ming Shen-Lin were listed as majority shareholders."

"They're makin' this too easy," said Gunner, who appeared to immediately regret his words. "My apologies, Irish."

"Not necessary, Gunner."

"A clear picture is beginning to appear," said Burns. "Kerr found someone easily manipulated to do his bidding. Ming Shen-Lin as well."

I turned around and saw that the room had gone silent and many of those who had previously been seated at their own tables were now gathered around the one where Burns Butler was holding court.

He motioned to Money to step forward. "While we may be able to piece together a likely scenario, the question foremost presenting itself is what our agenda will be even if we believe we uncover all the answers."

Money cleared his throat. "Since you're asking me directly, you are aware the only answer I can give is an official one."

Burns nodded.

"State would certainly have enough ammunition to propose a deal for Harris' extradition. The announcement that they've granted him asylum is out of character for Beijing. It would be more like them to simply grant it without admitting to it."

"Agreed."

"Which means they already know what they want in exchange."

"Go on."

From where I sat, I had a clear view of Dr. Benjamin when he stood and approached the table. I expected him to speak, but he didn't. He was, however, laser focused on Money.

"The most obvious answer is Jinyan."

"Out of the question," blurted Benjamin. All eyes turned toward him. "You cannot begin to consider such an exchange."

My eyes met Decker's; he raised a brow.

"Who is Jinyan?" asked Stella.

Rather than continuing to look at Dr. Benjamin, most in the room turned to Burns, who turned to me.

"Jinyan Yanli is a Hong Kong law professor and activist who was apprehended in what has been called the 701 Lockdown, during which more than three hundred 'dissidents' were arrested. The predawn raid took place on July 1, 1998—one year after the United Kingdom's official handover of Hong Kong to China."

Burns motioned for me to go on.

"After she spent ten years in an undisclosed detention center, tortured, and denied medical treatment for cancer, a human rights advocacy group appealed to the United Nations to intervene. She was eventually granted asylum in the US."

"She was tortured daily. Beaten close to death. They deprived her of sleep, withheld medication for both diabetes and cancer. She was blocked from receiving surgery and chemotherapy that may have saved her life." Dr. Benjamin spoke softly, his voice taut with emotion, yet there wasn't a person in the room who didn't hear every word he said.

"She has repeatedly asked that she be granted permission to return to Hong Kong so she may see her family once more before she dies," said Money.

"I'm sorry to be blunt, but if she is on her deathbed, why does China want her return?" asked Stella.

"Because then they win," said Gunner.

Dr. Benjamin shook his head. "It isn't Yanli they want." His eyes filled with tears.

Burns, whose eyes had been downcast, raised his head. "It's her son they want."

I looked from him to Adam Benjamin. "Your son."

His head barely moved, but I saw him nod.

"Where is he?" I asked.

"I don't know."

"When was the last you saw him?" I knew the answer before he gave it.

"Nine years ago."

"What if we brought him to her?" I asked.

Money shook his head. "There would be no opportunity for negotiation for Harris if that were to happen."

"Let's just go in and shoot the slimy bastard," said Gunner.

Both Doc and Money glared at him.

"What?" he said, looking between the two. "You can't tell me you're unaware that assassinations take place every fucking day of the year, McTiernan. Let's just be honest."

"Gunner," warned Doc. "You know how this works."

"We can't stop Yanli from going back to Hong Kong. If she makes that decision, it's out of our hands," said Money.

"You can't seriously be considering—"

Doc held up his hand, interrupting Dr. Benjamin. "What he's saying is if we want to make this negotiation, we have to act before she does."

Razor raised his hand. "Sorry to interrupt the current topic of conversation, but does the name Lam Shum mean anything to anyone?"

"What's the context?" Doc asked.

"He was secretary-general of Interpol from 1997 to 2007."

"Is that a lengthy tenure?" asked Stella.

Burns shook his head. "The position is appointed for a five-year term and may be reappointed once."

Razor was back to studying his computer. "According to their annual report, Interpol's operational support, aka funding through private donations, increased more than fifty percent in 1998. Similar growth occurred over the next five years. It leveled out in 2003."

"Money laundering," blurted Gunner.

I agreed. "The timing is perfect, given the handover."

"It's estimated that mainland China moves upwards of $100 billion in US dollars through Hong Kong annually," said Money. "Although there have been decreases since the establishment of AML/CFT, or Anti-Money Laundering and Counter-Terrorist Financing Ordinance."

Gunner's cough sounded more like "bullshit" than a hack.

"Are you fucking kidding me?" said Stella, causing all heads to turn in her direction. "All Kerr's bullshit about voluntary contributions being funneled through Interpol keeping the intelligence community and entire governments from crumbling, how the world would stop spinning without men like him making the power plays behind the scenes, was really all just about money laundering? Not that I bought into his altruistic diatribe for a split second, but fuck, I want to kill him all over again."

"You raise a good point," said Doc. "In terms of how he may have convinced Harris to 'do his bidding,' as someone else said. My guess is the young man became disillusioned by the agency, maybe even the government as a whole after we failed to take care of his father. Kerr swoops in, convinces him that Argead is dedicated to righting wrongs or whatever other bullshit he fed him. Even his 'code name' speaks to this. Xander, or Alexander the Great, believed himself to be the defender of the Argead."

Thoughts raced through my head. That first mission, when Dingo, 337, and Julius were gunned down, we'd been tasked with watching a Chinese-born Canadian national who was the kingpin of a drug network reportedly bringing in fifty million dollars annually. The assignment wasn't to bring him in. It was to figure out who in Hong Kong was laundering his money.

"You knew about the hit," I said, looking directly at Dr. Benjamin. "That's why you were there that night. You and your son."

When he didn't respond, I pushed back my chair. Burns put his hand on my arm.

"It was a part of an investigation, in the same way you have been conducting your own," said the doctor.

"My investigation was to find out who was murdering my fellow agents. I don't give a shit about who the fuck moves money where." I was shouting and I didn't care. "There is no goddamn greater good. These are human beings who have been murdered, their bodies left in the street in order to keep money flowing into the pockets of greedy power mongers." I pointed at Money. "And the agency covered it up. Burned the missions like they never happened. Why? Because motherfuckers like Fisk, Flatley—God knows who else—were on the receiving end of that cash?"

This time I did get up, but not to go after Benjamin. I stormed out of the room and out of the house.

"Irish." I heard Cope call my name, but I kept walking. "Paxon!" he shouted.

I spun around. "You are no better," I shouted. "You were going to let it happen to Malin Kilbourne. You were going to sacrifice her life as a means to an end. Fuck off, Cope!"

I had no idea where Flynn might be. She said she was off today, which meant she could've left the ranch like she had earlier this morning. Not knowing where else to go, I walked over to the corral, stood by the fence, and watched the horses. I was shocked when the one I'd ridden the one and only time I'd been on horseback sauntered over to me.

"I don't have any treats for you today, buddy," I said, rubbing his forehead like Flynn had taught me to do. He edged closer so the side of his face was right next to mine. It was the most natural thing in the world for me to lean into him. "Can't tell you how much I needed that," I said.

I felt a hand on my shoulder and immediately knew it was Flynn's. I turned and pulled her into my arms.

"How do you do it?"

"Do what?"

"Manage to appear when I need you the most?"

"You do the same for me."

"I do? I feel like this is one-sided."

"You were there when Trent called me a name in that bar. You were there to warn me away from that other guy. But mostly, Paxon, you were the first man who made me feel like I could be desired as a woman. There is nothing one-sided about what we do for each other."

Her mentioning Trent reminded me that Ink told me he'd been fired from the place in Redstone. He'd also muttered something about a broken nose that I chose not to follow up on for details.

I shook my head, willing the memory away. I smiled at Flynn and looked into her eyes. "When we first met, I remember thinking I wished I could be ten years younger, just so I would be closer in age to you. Now I realize it would only make you *another* ten years wiser than I am."

"What happened in there?" She motioned toward the house with her head.

"I have a different philosophy about life than most of the people I work with."

"How?"

"I don't believe in the greater good. I don't believe a life should be sacrificed in order to save the many."

"And yet it's how you live your own life."

"What do you mean?"

"You have repeatedly put yourself in danger for the sake of those many. I don't need to know the details of things you've done or been a part of since you went to work for the CIA. I still know you put your life on the line. Just like my brother Buck does. Probably everyone here in that room does."

"It's different when you make the choice yourself than it is when the decision is made for you."

"Those other agents did make that choice, Paxon. It was their own sacrifice, not yours or anyone else's on their behalf."

"I don't want to, but I should return to the meeting."

Flynn reached up and kissed me. "My offer never expires. If you need me, you know how to reach me."

"Why are you so good to me?"

"I think we already covered that. Now, go, so you can get done early enough that I can come to your cabin again tonight."

39

Irish

I could feel the tension in the room the moment I walked inside. It flowed particularly strong between Money and Dr. Benjamin. As I walked past their table, I made eye contact with both Emme and Lynx. Her furrowed brow led me to wonder if she was feeling the same thing I was.

I walked to the front of the room and waited for conversations to die down before I spoke.

"Thanks, everyone," I began when heads that had been facing away turned in my direction. "I'd like to bring us back to a vector view and get out of the weeds if we can."

I saw heads nodding.

"I can't speak for anyone else, but since I began this 'mission'—if you want to call it that—my personal mandate has remained the same: to find out why agents were being 'killed in the line of duty' at a rate that was exponentially higher than in previous years combined. Additionally, to get to the bottom of why those murders were being covered up by the CIA, the organization that the majority of the dead agents worked for. My personal mandate hasn't changed."

"Nor mine," said Cope when our eyes met.

"To be honest, I don't know that I thought much about the desired outcome besides stopping the carnage. Three months ago, when the initial rounds of arrests were made, I believed we caught the perpetrators and it was time to call the mission. It wasn't long before I realized how wrong I was." I took a deep breath and slowly let it out.

"I'm in the same place today. I listen as new discoveries bring yet another piece that fits into the puzzle. It would be easy to name Xander Harris as the culprit, but that would be as naive as thinking this…this…Argead was taken down with Fisk, or Flatley before him."

My eyes met Burns', and he nodded.

"What we have to determine now, collectively, is what we believe the desired outcome to be. Who are the players that remain that we know about? The quick answer is Harris, Antonov, and Chen. We all know there are layers upon layers deeper than that. So again, what is the desired outcome?"

"Why aren't we revisiting a deal with Fisk?" asked Cope.

"You're thinking now that Kerr and Byrne are dead, he might be willing to talk? Antonov and Chen are still alive and well, the last I heard."

"I don't know, Irish. I just think it might be worth another ask."

"It wouldn't hurt anything," said Doc.

"I need to know you aren't considering sacrificing Jinyan Yanli," said Benjamin.

"I don't think we've made a determination either way," said Money.

"I must insist—"

"As was just said, we haven't made a determination either way." As far as I was concerned, Dr. Benjamin was in no position to ask for anything. A case could be made that he was an accomplice to murder, given he admitted in front of a room full of people that he had been aware a hit was scheduled to take place and he stood by and watched it happen.

"I have information that may influence the extradition of Harris."

My patience with Dr. Benjamin was wearing thin enough that deferring to someone else was necessary. "Decker?"

He stood and walked toward the doctor. "Let's get something straight. We are a combined team working toward a common goal. Either you are on this team, or you're not. If you have an agenda that differs from that of the majority, you have no business being here."

When Saint stood, I anticipated things getting heated.

"Before we go any further, let's take a break. Decker, Dr. Benjamin, let's take this conversation offline."

When Decker motioned us outside, Saint followed.

"Irish? A moment?" he asked.

"What?" I snapped.

"I'd like a few minutes alone with Adam."

"It better be to tell him to either get with the program or get the fuck off this ranch," I seethed.

"It is neither, but I guarantee the same result."

I found his use of the word guarantee an interesting choice.

"Decker, let's give Saint and Dr. Benjamin a minute."

He looked at me like I had three heads, shook his, and then stalked inside with me following.

"Can I be of any assistance?" asked Emme.

I looked out the window to where the two men appeared to be in a heated debate. "I really don't know."

"I had no idea."

"Do you mean about the reason he's so obsessed with what is happening in Hong Kong?"

"Yes. He never let on."

"Did you expect him to?"

She shrugged. "There were times I felt as though he was baring his soul. I suppose he was, just not enough that I could understand what he was trying to tell me."

"What do you mean?"

"Essentially, what you said about his obsession with Hong Kong. My focus with China has always been single-minded, at least on a personal level. I want to put an end to the flow of pharmaceuticals and active ingredients from China into the United States. To the world, if I could influence it, but it has always been my goal to find a way to end our dependence on them for something that could so easily be used against us."

I knew Emme's older brother had died from prolonged use and a subsequent fatal dose of fentanyl, and that upon his death, she vowed to everything she just reiterated.

"Dr. Benjamin's goals aren't that different from mine. He wants to see change in a part of the world that will get far worse for anyone who is prodemocracy or speaks out against the Chinese government. I predict we will not see change for the good in our lifetime."

"It would've been nice if he communicated what he was doing or where he was going prior to leaving, but I suppose that's too much for Saint to consider," I said as I watched Saint and the doctor get into a vehicle.

"I know you've never cared for him, but I feel I must defend him."

I tried to remember a time in the past when Emme may have seen Saint and I interact, but I couldn't recall an occasion when we did.

"It's more in the way you talked about him," she said, nudging me.

"Or it's that you read minds."

"If I could, I never would've doubted you," she repeated what she'd said yesterday.

"You could look at it this way; I was better at my job than you thought."

She laughed, and so did I. It was a nice reminder of how much I'd enjoyed working with her when I first went undercover at MIT.

"Back to Saint. He's a good man, Paxon. I doubt Lynx and I would be together if it weren't for his interference."

"Interesting word choice."

She laughed again.

"Look, I appreciate what you're saying. However, from my perspective, maybe even Lynx's too, the man should probably consider a different career."

"Are you saying you don't believe he's effective in his role as an MI6 agent?"

"I doubt you'd find many who disagree with me."

"Perhaps not." When she walked away, Decker approached.

"Ready to get back to work?"

"In a minute." I went outside and Decker followed. "What I said earlier about not knowing the end game on this, I really don't. I suppose the only way we'll know how much deeper this goes is to get Harris and/ or Fisk to talk."

"Fisk we have; Harris we don't."

"Do we go in and get him or negotiate his release?"

"Fuck negotiation. We go in and get him the same way we went in and got Saint and Benjamin."

"Any idea where he's being kept?"

"This idea that the Chinese can hide where prisoners are being detained is nothing but a big crock of fucking propaganda. Name one, give me fifteen minutes, and I'll tell you where they're being held."

"Do you think they consider him a prisoner?"

"With everything he knows, they're keeping him alive for the sole purpose of making a deal. Once Jinyan dies, or someone else they want bad enough to trade him for, Xander dies too."

"That's no secret to Xander, then."

"Sure as shit isn't."

"Fisk knows it too."

"You got that right, Irish. He wasn't afraid of Kerr; it's China that terrifies him."

When I walked back inside, I saw Decker rub his hands together. "You aren't going," I said over my shoulder.

"I know," he grumbled. "I'll sure as hell be watching from home, though."

I approached Money first, who by the time I got to him had already started packing up his computer. "About time. I thought I was going to be forced to suggest leaving myself. Better that I don't know the details than if I have to run this up the chain of command."

"I'm going to ask Dr. Charles, err, Edgemon to step out as well."

"Understood."

Money put his hand on my shoulder. "Godspeed, Irish."

At the same time I walked Money and Emme out, Saint drove up.

"Where's Dr. Benjamin?" I asked when he got out of the SUV.

"Making contact with Jinyan."

"You should go with them," I said, pointing to the vehicle Money had just unlocked.

"Why?"

"Because what's about to happen in there is need-to-know."

"You're going in."

I had no reaction.

"I need to go with you."

Interesting word choice. "Need?"

"Yes, Irish. Need."

"I can't help you, Saint." I turned to go inside.

"Wait."

I sighed. "What?"

"I will agree to any role you choose."

"What's this all about, Saint?"

"I've left MI6."

"And?"

"This is what I do, Irish. I am presently a man with no purpose."

"Maybe you should take a moment to reflect on how you got in this situation."

"I left MI6 of my own accord. I was not asked to leave."

"Why?"

"For the same reason many of the men inside that room left the CIA or Lynx left MI6 as I did. I was tired of my hands being perpetually tied. Tired of the bureaucracy that came along with the job. Do you realize I have been Benjamin's bloody caretaker for the past three years?"

"I don't know…"

"There was a time in your life when people believed you were someone you're not. I was there when the men and women in that room showed you their support. I saw the look on your face. Allow me this one chance to prove I am not the man you believe I am."

"Fuck," I said under my breath.

"What?"

"It isn't hard to see how you were able to seduce those millions of women you've bedded."

"As I said, you know how it feels to have people believe you're someone you're not."

"Let me ask you something."

"Go on."

"At one point, Lynx said you were with Emme. Is that true?"

"To me, she was Charlie, and to her, I was Tommy. As far as being with her, tell me, Irish, didn't you fall a little bit in love with her yourself?"

"Hard not to."

"Precisely." He looked out at the ranch and then at me. "As hard as this was for me to accept at one point in time, Lynx is the man she was always meant to be with. And before you ask, our dear, sweet Dr. Charles was as clueless of my affections as she is brilliant in so many other ways."

When we went inside, it was evident Decker had made the announcement that we were going to extract Harris.

Like I saw Deck do earlier, Gunner was rubbing his hands together like a child waiting to open a Christmas present.

Doc motioned me over. "I'll be honest, it isn't easy for any of us not to take charge and plan this extraction. However, we're following your lead. I will, however, offer the use of any of the K19 fleet of planes."

"Fleet, what a crock of shit," mumbled Decker, joining us.

"I'd appreciate it if we could walk through this before announcing it to the entire group."

"Roger that," said Doc, motioning for Razor and Gunner to take a hike.

He, Deck, and I sat down.

"I'm going to be equally honest. I've never run an extraction mission. Correction. I've never been on an extraction mission."

"You trained for it; it'll come back to you. Plus, you'll have the best of the best by your side. We won't let you fuck up too bad," said Deck.

"I hope you're including K19 in that group," said Doc.

"You know I am, especially since I can't come along. Mila—"

"Say no more," said Doc. "Even if you said you wanted to go, no one in this room would allow it."

I chuckled at the look on Decker's face. As if he'd permit anyone to say no to him—except maybe Mila.

"He's here," he said, pointing to a map on his computer screen.

"Shanghai?" I asked.

Decker zoomed in. "Within Gongqing Forest Park, along the Huangpu River, there are at least three 'cottages' used as hei jianyu or black jails."

I'd heard the term that referred to a network of detention centers established by Chinese security forces and private security companies where detainees were held without trial, often without knowing the reason for their incarceration. As seen on the screen, many of these facilities looked like cottages; some were even set up within hotels. Regardless of what they looked like on the outside, within, they were referred to as the "alleyways to hell."

Since they were often manned by private security personnel, there was no oversight of treatment. According to many human rights activists, the majority of the guards were hired specifically for their sadistic personalities.

Someone like Harris would likely have believed he was being given a home in the forest where he would be protected twenty-four seven. Instead, it was plausible that he was beaten, deprived of food and sleep, and even of medical attention if it was required.

Decker outlined what he believed would be the quickest and safest way in and out.

Two teams would fly from Los Angeles to Taiwan. From there, seaplanes—the riskiest part of the mission other than the extraction itself—would transport us over the China Sea to the archipelago Zhoushan. Once there, we would travel by car to Gongqing.

Total travel time would be almost forty-eight hours there and back for an extraction planned to take less than fifteen minutes.

"We'll leave at zero six hundred tomorrow and depart six hours later out of Los Angeles," said Doc. "While we're in the air, we'll review the extraction op Decker and Gunner are preparing for us."

"Do you need me to be a part of that?" I asked Decker.

"If you would like to be, it's your call. However, no offense, Irish, but I don't even need Gunner's help."

"Bullshit," he said, pulling out a chair and sitting down. "I'm the one who doesn't need you."

"Come on," said Doc, motioning for me to follow. "These two will go at it all night if they have an audience."

40

Flynn

Is it still early? said the text Paxon sent.

It's four in the afternoon, I responded.

Where are you?

Sitting on the porch swing, waiting for you.

Be right there.

I didn't tell him I wasn't alone. He'd find that out soon enough.

When the black SUV pulled up, two men got out. I was as shocked to see Paxon arrive with Saint as he probably was to see Dr. Benjamin seated beside me.

Saint picked up his pace so he was the first to walk up the steps. "Flynn," he said.

"Hi," I responded, looking beyond him at Paxon's puzzled expression.

"Adam? What are you doing here?"

"I went for a walk…"

"He got a little lost," I answered for him.

The expression on Paxon's face didn't change as he walked closer. I shook my head, just slightly, and he nodded.

"She's gone."

"I'm sorry," said Saint, reaching forward to put his hand on the man's arm.

Saint looked over his shoulder at Paxon, who turned around and walked back to the SUV. When he got inside, I could see he made a phone call.

"Let's get you to the cabin, and we'll make arrangements—"

"I need to go to her."

"Understood," said Saint, helping him up from the swing. "Who told you?"

"The nurse."

I stood too. "Can I give you a hug before you go?"

Dr. Benjamin turned to me, and we embraced briefly before Saint escorted him to the same vehicle Paxon had gotten into. He held up his index finger, which I took as meaning he'd be right back.

I felt so awful for the man I found walking aimlessly down the dirt road that led to the three cabins where our guests were staying.

"Can I help?" I'd asked, pulling up beside him.

"I believe I took a wrong turn."

"Well, climb on in, and I'll get you to wherever you were headed." I never found out where that had been because when he started talking, I drove to the closest place I could think of where we could sit and I could listen to him.

He told me the story of how he'd met the woman who was the love of his life and how, even though they couldn't be together because of what they both did for a living, they'd never loved anyone else—except for the son they shared that, until earlier today, no one knew was his.

A few minutes later, the SUV returned. This time, Paxon was the only person in it.

"Hey," he said, walking up and sitting beside me.

"Hey." I rested my head on his shoulder.

"He said you picked him up on the side of the road."

"Inside the ranch, but yes. The woman he loved died."

"I heard."

"You have something else to talk to me about, though, don't you?"

Paxon turned and looked into my eyes. "I have to leave."

"Okay."

"First thing tomorrow."

I nodded, unsure what to say.

"Can you stay?"

"With you tonight?" I asked.

"Yes."

"Of course."

Paxon stood, took my hand, and led me inside.

41

Irish

Of course I wished Flynn and I could make love tonight. There wasn't another woman in the world I wanted to be with, could be with, but neither of us was ready. We hardly knew each other. And yet, somewhere deep inside, it felt as though I'd known her forever.

"Just so you know, I won't ask where you're going."

"If you did, I couldn't tell you."

"There's another question I want to ask."

"Go ahead."

She shook her head. "Maybe later."

"There are so many things I want to say to you."

Flynn smiled. "Go ahead," she repeated my words. "Maybe later."

"Paxon? Can you just hold me?"

I led her into the bedroom. "Is this okay with you?"

"It is."

Flynn put her hand in mine, and I led her over to the bed. We both lay on it, facing each other in the same way we had last night on the floor in front of the fireplace. I looked into her eyes, wishing I was better at putting the right words together to tell her how I felt.

"I want you to know how much these last few days, these last hours in particular, have meant to me."

She pulled away and her brow furrowed, but I tightened my grip so she was close enough that I could kiss her.

"Paxon—"

"Shh." I put my fingertips on her lips. "I'm not saying goodbye or telling you we can only be friends. I just really suck at this."

She smiled. "Just say how you feel."

Could I? If I did, would I sound insane?

"Just do it," she whispered, brushing my lips with hers.

I rolled over and looked up at the ceiling. There were a hundred things I wanted to say, all at once, and yet I couldn't get a single one out.

"I'm not sure how long I'll be gone, and when I return, I don't know where I'll be going next." Did that even make sense?

"Where do you want to go?"

"I'd love to come back here—"

Flynn kissed me. Not just a lip brush, an actual kiss. When her tongue pushed into my mouth, I pushed too.

I gathered her into my arms and rolled so her body rested on mine.

"Did I say the wrong thing?" I asked when she pulled away and rested her head on my chest.

"No. The exact right thing, actually."

I laughed. "Which was?"

"That you'd love to come back here. And before you say 'but,' that's why I kissed you. To stop you from saying it."

"Flynn—"

This time, she put her fingers on my lips. "Look, I know how your life works. I've seen it firsthand with my brother. I know I may not ever see you again, but for tonight, I want to pretend that I will."

"It isn't that I don't want to."

"I know, Paxon."

"What I'm about to say will sound like the most selfish thing you've ever heard, but I went a very long time without comfort in my life. Today, when all I needed was that, you gave it to me. It was the most precious gift, and I'll never forget that."

"I'm going to ask something of you."

"Go ahead."

"Comfort me now, Paxon."

I drew her into my arms and ran my hands up and down her back. She raised her face and kissed me.

"I want more," she whispered.

I didn't need to ask what she meant. It was obvious by the way she moved against me. Her body responded instinctively, but that didn't mean either one of us was ready for more.

"Paxon?"

I put my hands on either side of her face and looked into her eyes. "As much as I want to feel your bare skin against mine, I don't want to rush this. You mean something to me, Flynn. When the time is right, for both of us, there will be more."

Her cheeks were bright red, and she tried to look away.

"Flynn, please. I want to do the right thing."

She wrapped her fingers around my wrist and brought my right hand to rest on her breast.

I shuddered, feeling the pebbled nipple against my palm. My cock throbbed with want, but my mind had to prevail.

"Just this," she whispered, unfastening the buttons on her blouse. "When you leave, I want to remember your touch. Give me that, Paxon."

I shifted my body and sat up. When Flynn did the same, I reached around and unfastened her bra. She let it and her blouse slide off her body.

"Just this," I said, taking my time learning the curves of the upper half of her body. I didn't stop with her breasts; I kissed her mouth, the side of her neck, the soft skin on the inside of her elbow.

Flynn whimpered and mewled; they were the most beautiful sounds I'd ever heard. I'd give anything to remove the clothes—hers and mine—that were a barrier between us. Anything except the hurt and confusion I knew she'd feel when I had to leave before dawn.

Our kisses were harder, deeper, softer, sweeter, more impassioned than any I'd experienced in my life.

"There's something I need to say, and it won't be easy."

Her eyes filled with tears.

"I'm sorry, Flynn, but I must say it."

"It's okay."

I held her tight to me. "If I don't come back, I want you to know that this has been the most important night of my life. I've never known how it felt to be so torn about leaving. I never knew how hard it was to leave a loved one behind when called for a mission. I couldn't empathize with the men and women I worked with, because I'd never felt it for myself. As important as this mission is to me, as much as I've sacrificed in my life to see it through, I do not want to leave you. It's tearing me up inside."

"I will be here when you get back, Paxon. Every time, I'll be waiting for you."

"And if I don't?"

"Then I will treasure the gifts you've given me. I'll remember your hands on my body and so much more than that. How it felt when you first held me and we danced. The look on your face when you told me how pretty I looked. The desire I see in your eyes right now. I'll remember it all for the rest of my life."

When she put her hands on the hem of my shirt, I pulled it over my head. We slept on and off that way. Both of us naked from the waist up. When she turned her back to my front, I rested both hands on her breasts. Like her, I wanted to remember how it felt once I was gone.

It felt as though only minutes had passed when the alarm on my phone signaled it was time for me to get ready to leave.

"Is it okay if I stay here awhile?" she asked.

How I wanted to ask her not to leave until I returned—to be waiting for me in the bed we shared.

I wrapped a blanket around her shoulders and walked to the front door of the cabin with her by my side.

"You mean so much to me. I hope you know that, Flynn."

"I more than know it, Paxon. I feel it."

"I feel it too."

* * *

She was on my mind during the flight to California, even while Decker and Gunner outlined each carefully planned step of the op during which we'd extract William "Xander" Harris from the black jail cottage where Decker was certain he was being kept.

I thought about her as we walked into Doc's Montecito home, just outside Santa Barbara, where we picked up tactical gear and the weapons that would be necessary to execute this phase of the mission that had been part of my life for so long that there were times I couldn't remember what it had felt like before. Except when I was with Flynn. Then, I remembered.

More, I longed for it to be over. Once it was, I had no idea what I'd do with my life other than spend as much of it with her as she'd let me.

When we left for the airfield, Decker accompanied us. Instead of getting on the plane we'd be taking to

Taiwan, he boarded a smaller aircraft that would transport him to Texas.

"Godspeed," he said, shaking each of our hands. I was last and he embraced me. "Let's end this, Irish. Once and for all."

My eyes met Saint's when right before he boarded, he gave me a head nod. While they'd said it was my decision, I made certain Doc was comfortable with the former MI6 agent accompanying him, Razor, Gunner, Lynx, and I on this side of the mission.

Those remaining at Roaring Fork Ranch would be working with Money to develop a new offer for former Director Fisk in the hope that whatever information we couldn't get out of Harris, we'd get from him.

I slept as much as my brain would allow me during the thirteen-hour flight, knowing I would need to be well rested for what came after we landed.

When I couldn't sleep, I reviewed each step we were about to take as they were outlined. I looked up when Gunner sat beside me. It had changed since Decker initially talked about it. He and Gunner had modified the original plan to eliminate travel on land as much as possible.

"We get in, we get out, and we bring everyone home with us. While this may be your first extraction, it isn't the first time you've relied on your gut to get you through a mission."

"Copy that."

"I have a question for you."

"Go ahead."

"How badly do you want this fucker brought back alive?"

"I can't answer that. I've been weighing that question over and over in my own mind. Knowing what he's been responsible for facilitating, it will be difficult for me not to kill him myself. What we need from him, though, if we can get him to give it to us, is crucial to us ending this—once and for all."

"Roger that. I'll do my best not to get trigger-happy, but it ain't gonna be easy."

42

Irish

With any op, we planned for success but were prepared for what to do when the worst happened. Even in the midst of it, I felt like I was outside my body, watching its execution being carried out by someone else.

Once we were in the seaplane, I looked down at the East China Sea, mesmerized by the way the water ebbed and flowed, even so far from a shoreline.

We landed in the river off Zhoushan, under the cover of the night sky, and loaded onto the boats that would take us from there, up the Yangtze to the Huangpu River. I looked out at the shoreline of the country that I'd seen for so long as the land of my enemy. I'd stopped seeing it as a place of homes and families. A place where generations of people lived and worked, from birth to death, most never believing an entire nation could be their enemy. Even their own.

"He better fucking be here," I heard Gunner mutter under his breath when the boat he and I were in came close enough to the shore that we could get out and execute the most important—and most dangerous—part of the entire mission.

As we crept through the heavy forest and it came into view, the place where we believed Xander was being kept looked, as Decker predicted, like a simple cottage—except for the heavy bars covering the doors and windows that I could see through my night-vision goggles.

As we approached, I used a hand-held Doppler radar device that would determine the number of people inside and whether there was any movement. According to what I saw on the screen, there were three and none were doing anything more than breathing.

We rounded the house to where Decker had said we'd find a window leading into a crawl space just beneath an area adjacent to the room where the radar showed a single person.

Gunner, known as the grand master of stealth, was tasked with extracting Harris while the rest of us provided cover both inside and out. Doc and Razor followed him in.

From where Saint and I stood by the entry point, I heard two quick pfooots—the sound of guns equipped with silencers being fired. I looked at the radar device and saw that there was no movement from the two bodies that had been in the other area of the house.

Seconds later, Gunner came out, carrying who I assumed was Harris in his arms.

"Go, go, go," I heard him shout through my earpiece as the rest of us scattered into the forest on our way to where Lynx waited with the boat.

I could see the water's edge when I heard shots being fired.

"Keep going," Saint shouted at me, spinning around with his gun drawn.

"Fuck, no!" I shouted back. I could see the movement of two people in the forest and shot in their direction as I continued running backward toward the boat.

"Bloody fucking hell!" I heard Saint yell right before I saw him go down.

While still firing, I raced over and grabbed his arm. "Can you walk?"

"Negative. Got hit in the leg."

I holstered my gun and picked him up using the fireman's carry. "Cover us," I shouted to Razor and Doc as I raced to the boat.

"Leg wound," I told Gunner when he helped me get Saint inside and seated so I could check the bleeding. It was minimal which meant the bullet hadn't hit an artery.

"Move out!" Razor shouted, jumping into the boat, behind Doc. Lynx went full throttle while the two men stood near at the aft, continuing to fire at those on the shore, picking them off one by one.

"Change the departure location," Gunner shouted at Razor.

"Roger that."

I heard him contact the pilot of the seaplane and tell him to meet us at the mouth of the Yangtze River, which was seventy-five nautical miles closer than Zhoushan.

I looked over at Gunner, who appeared to be checking Harris' vitals. "Is he alive?"

"Just barely."

"Jinyan's death must've been leaked," said Doc.

Gunner shook his head. "Or the people guarding him hated the fucker as much as I do."

Doc, who was given his code name because he was a physician's assistant, asked Gunner to move out of his way. "We need him to stay alive at least long enough to interrogate him," I heard him say under his breath.

* * *

During the flight on the seaplane as well as the flight to the US on the K19 jet, Doc continued to monitor Harris' condition after he removed the bullet from Saint's leg and stitched him up.

"How is he?" I asked when Saint came out of the stateroom, limping but otherwise appearing uninjured.

"If you mean Harris, Doc said it would be touch and go. He's got a saline IV going along with administering pain meds."

"Fuck the pain meds," grumbled Gunner. "It's one thing to keep the bastard alive. It's another to keep him pain free."

"We need to talk about what the plan will be after we arrive back in the States," I said when Doc stepped out of the stateroom.

"Burns is setting that up now. We'll keep Harris on the West Coast temporarily. Once we've accomplished our part of the interrogation, we'll let Money take over."

Which meant that until we were finished, regardless of how long that might take, our return to the US had to remain classified. There would be no way for me to alert Flynn I was in the States, let alone try to see her.

In the back of my mind, I knew this was a possibility. That didn't do anything to assuage the disappointment I felt knowing I'd be a two-hour flight away from her and unable to communicate even by text.

* * *

We established a base on the Central Coast of California after we arrived in the States. K19 kept a safe house in a place called Harmony, just south of a town called Cambria, where Razor and Gunner owned a duplex that sat on the bluffs overlooking the Pacific Ocean.

We established a rotating schedule so there were a minimum of two people in Harmony with Harris at all times. When we weren't, we'd take turns catching sleep while also monitoring the fallout from Xander's extraction. As was typical with China, there was no chatter whatsoever about the man they'd recently announced to the world they'd granted asylum to.

The fact that they'd made the announcement initially was, as Money had said, designed to let the US know they were open to negotiation for his release.

Doc continued monitoring the man's care. After remaining critical for several days, he finally announced that while Harris wasn't completely out of danger, he was ready to downgrade him to serious.

We were one step closer to beginning the interrogations we'd spent several days crafting. The single most important piece of information we needed to get out of Xander was how much of the Argead network remained functional. We all agreed it would be the thing he'd be least willing to give up.

On our sixth day in California, I received a call from Burns Butler. "Hello, sir," I answered.

"Irish, I want you to know that my wife, Sorcha, has been pestering our oldest son endlessly about when you will be available for a visit to our ranch. Kade, knowing he is no match for his mother's tenacity, has agreed to give you up for the afternoon tomorrow."

"I'm sorry to be the cause of trouble, sir."

"On the contrary. 'Tis Sorcha who is relentless in her pursuit of an audience with you. I'll advise you to come on an empty stomach as she'll prepare a feast in your honor that she will insist you gorge yourself on."

"Laird!" I heard a woman's voice shout in the background.

"Oh dear. I've been found out. Kade will brief you on your transport, and we very much look forward to seeing you tomorrow."

As it happened, Doc and I were on duty together at the Harmony house when the call came in. I sheepishly went looking for him after it ended.

"I'm sorry," I began, but he raised his hand.

"Please, I'm the one who should apologize. You have risen to the role of godlike-superhero status with my mother, and she will not let up until she's had her audience with you."

"I didn't do anything anyone else wouldn't have done."

"As Gunner says far too often, bullshit." Doc laughed, and so did I. "Listen, Irish, you did good. When someone says 'thank you,' say 'you're welcome.'"

"Burns said you'd brief me on transportation tomorrow."

"Right. My brother Naughton will pick you up. I'll text you the directions to the helipad. It's right outside Cambria."

"Helipad?"

"Like I said, just say 'you're welcome.'"

43

Flynn

"Believe me, plane travel for normal people is nothing like this," said Stella when we boarded the small plane.

"Thank you for coming with me."

"Look at this," she said, waving her arm. "Who wouldn't have offered to accompany you."

"You have to be away from Buck, though."

"I'm only staying until you're safely delivered, and then I'm turning right around and coming back."

I looked in the direction of the rear of the plane, where Ink sat. There was no question of whether I'd be safe. Terrified out of my wits about flying was a whole different story.

44

Irish

Doc offered to give me a lift to the helipad, saying there was something he wanted to discuss with me.

"You'd think the ranch was hours away. Honestly, I could've driven you there in less time than it will take the helicopter to land, you to get on board, and for it to take off again. And before you say anything, the wrath I'd face from my mother if I did that is what prevented me from suggesting it."

I looked out the window at the view of the Pacific Ocean. I hadn't spent much time on the West Coast, but I certainly understood why Doc, Gunner, and Razor kept homes there.

He pulled off the main road and drove down what looked more like a dirt path. He stopped by an open field and cut the engine.

"Irish, I'm going to make you an offer you don't have to accept. All I ask is that you hear me out before you make a decision one way or another."

I couldn't help but think he was about to offer me a job. I was certainly willing to hear him out. Making a decision about anything to do with my future wasn't something I was prepared to do.

He turned his head to face me. "You've given up a quarter of your life to this mission. As someone who did the same for most of my life, not to one mission but to many, I want to share with you what it took me far too long to learn."

"Okay."

"Two things. First, you don't have to do it all. You have a team around you—two, in fact—who are willing to step up. Second, there is a life outside of work waiting for you. It is worth running as fast as you can in that direction. Seize whatever happiness is offered to you. No excuses. No delays. No putting anything else first. Take it by the reins and hold on tight. It's a helluva ride. Sometimes rough but always worth it."

"You mentioned you wanted me to wait until you were finished to make a decision."

"Right." Doc rubbed the back of his neck with his hand. "Irish, I want you to walk away and let us finish this." Before I could even open my mouth to respond, he put his hand on my arm. "You're too close. Worse, you feel as though every death of every agent sits heavily on your shoulders. None of them do, Irish. Not a single one. This isn't about the glory of finally ending the reign of terror of Argead and everyone associated with it. This is about it already being over. Let the cleaners come in and do their job. After that, let the judges ensure justice is served."

"You want me to walk away?"

He shook his head. "The battle is won. I feel it in my bones the same as you do. Whatever we learn from Harris or even Fisk, won't be much different than we already know it to be. There are three or four loose ends, but those are easily tied up. In fact, I'm pretty sure two already are. Lemme look." He pulled out his phone and swiped the screen before handing it to me.

The intelligence brief that appeared on the screen confirmed that Kim Ha-joon, secretary-general of Interpol, had been killed when the helicopter he was traveling in crashed upon takeoff.

"Maybe now wasn't the best time for me to show you that," he said, pointing to where one was about to land not far from where we were parked.

"You said there were two you believed were tied up."

"The second one is harder for me to confirm. However, I can tell you that Boris Antonov has a lot of explaining to do after the head of United Russia received compromising photos of his wife cavorting with his heir apparent."

I thought back to when Ali made reference to a brief she'd received predicting that Antonov would take over when his boss announced his retirement. I shook my head and wondered if the photos were even real. Either way, it didn't matter.

"That leaves Fisk and Harris. If I can talk Money into giving me ten minutes alone in a room with Fisk, I guarantee he'll tell us everything we want to know."

"Maybe Cope's father could help facilitate that."

"Maybe, or at least look the other way."

"I don't know him well, but something tells me Money wouldn't have the balls to take it up the chain of command, let alone deliver him to you without permission."

"I thought you knew," said Doc, swiping his phone's screen a second time. This time, he read what appeared to me. "In a press conference yesterday afternoon, on behalf of the president, Senator Henry Clay Copeland, chair of the Senate Select Committee on Intelligence, announced the appointment of Kellen McTiernan as the next director of the Central Intelligence Agency."

"I have to admit I'm stunned."

"He's a good man, Irish. Not like his recent predecessors."

"I hope you're right."

"I always am, just like Decker." Doc laughed. "I want you to think about what I said."

I watched as the blades of the helicopter slowed. "I'm not sure I can just let it go."

"You wouldn't be. You'd be letting your team wrap up the end of the mission on your behalf."

I looked out at the ocean. "I have no idea what I'm going to do once this is over."

"I can tell you that at least three job offers will be waiting whenever you're ready to consider them. And if anyone offers you something better than K19 does, just let me know and I'll double it."

I laughed, but he didn't. "You're serious?"

"Damn straight, I am. And if Ashford tries to top me, I'll triple it. Hell, I'll give up my own salary to keep you from going to work for him." Doc put his hand on my shoulder. "I won't pressure you to answer me now. Think it over while you're at my family's ranch and give me your answer by the end of the day."

"Is that any less pressure?"

"As I said a few minutes ago, seize whatever happiness is offered to you. Now go on before my mother calls to find out why you aren't there yet."

"You must be Irish," said the man who got out of the helicopter and waved at Doc before he drove away. "I'm Naughton."

"Nice to meet you, and thanks for this."

"Don't thank me. I never get the chance to fly this thing. In fact, if there's anywhere else you want to go before we head to the ranch, just say the word."

"I don't suppose this thing would get me to Colorado."

"You're right, it won't, but one of my brother's planes probably could."

I doubted I could go even if I wanted to. Until Harris was well enough to be questioned, there was still the matter of no one knowing we'd returned to the States. I looked over at Doc's brother. Obviously, his family knew. Maybe later I'd ask Doc if we could read Buck in. If so, I would do everything I could to get back to Flynn.

"It's a quick flight," Naughton said, handing me a headset. "But it's a beautiful one. I'll fly you past a couple of local landmarks that are only a little out of the way."

The first was Hearst Castle, which I'd heard of but never visited. "Believe me, it is way more impressive from up here than it is walking through it," he said as he circled around to go down the coast.

"That's Morro Rock you see off in the distance. Something else that is better seen from the sky than on foot. Let's just say that seals aren't very good housekeepers."

"It really is spectacular from up here. All of it." I waved my hand in the direction of the rolling hills we were flying over.

"We'll be at the ranch in about fifteen. Relax and enjoy the rest of the ride."

"That was quick," I said when we landed.

"Kade probably warned you that our mother was anxious to meet you; otherwise, I might've shown you a few more of the sights."

"I can't wait to meet her."

Naughton laughed. "I hope he warned you not to eat before you came."

"He did. So did your father."

I removed the headset and handed it to him.

"Listen, I don't know a lot of detail about what my brother does. Hell, up until a couple of years ago, I thought my father was nothing besides a vineyard owner who liked to dabble in technology. But I do know that my parents are laying out the red carpet for you. So whatever it is you've done, I want to thank you for your service."

I wasn't sure what to say, and then I thought about something Doc had said earlier. "You're welcome."

When the blades wound down and I climbed out, I saw someone who looked familiar walking toward me.

"Stella? What are you doing here?"

She walked up and put her arm through mine. "I heard you and I have been relieved of duty."

"Oh yeah? I thought Doc was going to let me decide for myself."

"I think you'll agree once you see the present I brought you."

"Did you get me my own airplane so I can fly back to Colorado?"

"Sadly, no. But once you see what it is, I doubt you'll want to anyway."

"You're right." I removed my arm from Stella's and rushed toward the best gift life had given me as I saw her walking toward me. "Flynn," I said, pulling her into my arms.

"Surprise!"

"I'd ask what you're doing here or how you got here, but I don't care. All that matters is that you're in my arms. I missed you so much." I put my hands on either

side of her face and kissed her again and again. "Do
you know how much I want to be alone with you?"

"I feel the same way, but this was actually Sorcha's
idea, so you at least have to meet her." Flynn took my
hand and led me in the direction of the house. "You'll
love her, by the way."

"There he is," said a woman with a Scottish accent
who I had no doubt was Doc's mother.

"Mrs. Butler, it's a pleasure to meet you." When I
held out my hand, she swatted it away.

"My name is Sorcha, and we hug in my house."

"I told you," mouthed Flynn. "Isn't she great?"

"Come and we'll eat, and you can tell me all about
how you conquered the evil Argead."

Burns approached and put his hand on my shoulder.
"Welcome to Butler Ranch, and don't say you weren't
duly warned."

"Listen, before you get started, I need to be on my
way," said Stella. "You like your surprise, right?"

I shook my head. "I love it."

Stella put her hand on my cheek. "This is what you
look like when you're happy. It looks good on you,
Irish."

"It looks good on you too."

"We'll catch up soon, at the Roaring Fork."

She said goodbye to Burns and Sorcha and then rushed out the door. "Flynn, see if you can get a helicopter ride while you're here!" We watched as she ran over to where Naughton waited.

"The plane ride was thrilling enough. I'm not sure I'm ready to ride in one of those."

"You'd love it. Naughton took me over the ocean on our way here."

Flynn's eyes opened wide. "The ocean? Is it far from here?"

"It's less than a half hour's drive, lass," said Sorcha, taking both of our hands and leading us over to the table. "Have you not seen it?"

"Never."

Doc's mother put her hand on Flynn's cheek. "Something tells me you're going to be seeing quite a lot of it in the days to come."

"Does she know something I don't?" I whispered in Flynn's ear.

She shrugged. "I was going to ask you the same thing."

I had no idea how much time had passed while Flynn and I sat at the table, talking to Burns and Sorcha. The entire time, I either held Flynn's hand or had my arm around her shoulders.

When she excused herself to use the restroom and Burns left the room too, Sorcha got up and came over to sit beside me.

"You love her, don't you?" She put her hand on my cheek that I was sure was bright red.

I leaned forward. "I think I should tell her first, don't you?"

She sat back in the chair and clapped her hands. "I knew it."

"Sorcha," said Burns, shaking his finger at her. "What are you up to?"

She stood and grabbed his hand. "Hush, you, and help me clean up the kitchen."

I got up to help too.

"Not you," she said over her shoulder. "It's a lovely time of day for you and Flynn to take a walk in the vineyards."

"Would you like to?" I asked when I saw her come around the corner.

"Are you sure we can't help?"

"Go on now, lass. You helped cook. We'll take care of this."

"I knew you had," I said once she and I were out on the porch.

"You did not."

"Yes, I did. I could even tell you which part."

"Okay, Mr. Smarty, what did I help with?"

"You made the cornbread and the chili."

Flynn laughed. "You just knew it wasn't my potato salad."

"Or coleslaw."

"Isn't it beautiful here?" she asked as we walked from the porch to the gravel path that wound through the vineyard.

I stopped walking and pulled her into me. "You're beautiful," I said before kissing her. "I wanted to do that at least a hundred times while we sat at that table."

"I did too." She kissed me back.

We walked toward the sunset and stopped when we came to a bench.

"Wow," Flynn gasped, taking in the view.

We sat quietly until we couldn't see the sun any longer.

"How long are you staying?" I asked.

"Me?"

I laughed. "Yeah, you."

"I have no idea. I thought maybe you did."

"I didn't even know you'd be here. I mean, I'm thrilled that you are." I pulled her close to me when I saw chill bumps on her arms. "Let's go back to the house and see if Burns or Sorcha know."

"Sorcha will know," said Flynn, laughing. "I don't think anything happens in the world without her knowing about it."

"There you are," said Sorcha when we came inside. "Naughton will be here soon. Laird has brought your things." She motioned to a small suitcase and then walked closer to me and took both my hands in hers.

"Paxon, I want you to let Stella write your story. The world deserves to know it."

"I think she'll write it with my permission or without it, not that it's my story alone, to begin with."

"It is and she won't. Tell her you want her to, and she will."

I studied her, not sure what to make of the formidable woman whose grasp on my hands was so tight and radiated so much warmth. It was easy to see Doc in both her and in Burns. He was the best of both of them.

"Promise me."

"I'll talk to her."

Sorcha beamed. "Good." She turned around and took Flynn's hands like she had mine. "Laird is bringing a basket of food for you to take on your journey."

"Thank you." Flynn looked over at me and then at Sorcha. "Um, do you know where we're going?"

"Only the first place. After that, it's up to the two of you."

"Where are we going tonight?"

She patted my cheek. "You'll see."

Flynn gasped when she saw the helicopter approach and land. "Are we going in that?"

"You'll love it, I promise."

45

Flynn

Instead of sitting in the one front passenger seat, Paxon sat next to me in the second row.

"There's still enough light that I can show you some of the coast before we land," said Naughton, who I'd met earlier when he picked Stella and me up from the airport and drove us to the ranch.

"I guess you know where we're going," Paxon joked.

"Let's just say I know where you're going first. After that, it's up to the two of you."

"Your mom said the same thing."

"Ready?"

I grabbed both of Paxon's hands when I felt us leaving the ground, and squeezed my eyes shut.

"Open," I heard him say through the headset. "You don't want to miss this."

The helicopter didn't go up too high, which meant we had a great view of the vineyards. "Look, there's our bench," I said, loosening my death grip on Paxon's hands. "Oh my gosh," I gasped when we went over a crest and I saw nothing but water on the horizon. My eyes filled with tears. Of course I'd seen photos, but nothing came close to the real thing. Not that it even looked real from up in the air.

"It's breathtaking," I said, looking over at Paxon.

He stroked my cheek with his thumb. "You are."

"I can swing by the rock so Flynn can see it if you'd like."

"That would be great," Paxon responded.

"The rock?"

He smiled. "You'll see."

When Naughton veered to the left, my stomach sunk like I was on a roller coaster. Paxon pointed.

"What is that?"

"Morro Rock," Naughton answered. "As I told your boyfriend, it's a much better view from up here than it is from the ground."

Wow. Naughton called Paxon my boyfriend. My first boyfriend. God, I loved the sound of that. "What's on it?" I asked. I could see movement but couldn't make out what it was.

"Seals. Thousands and thousands of seals. A little farther up the coast, you'll see sea lions. They smell even worse than those things do."

"I guess that's why it's better to see them from up here."

"You got it."

As we continued our tour, I studied Paxon as much as the scenery. There was something different about him since he left Colorado. If anyone asked, I wasn't sure I could describe it. He seemed lighter, certainly happier. I wanted to ask him what had happened wherever he went, but I knew I couldn't. The other thing was, I didn't want to bring it up for fear I'd remind him of something that would make him sad again.

"Are you flying over the castle?" Paxon asked.

"Nope. Gotta get you to your lodging while there's still enough light for you to see it."

The same thing happened to my stomach when I felt the helicopter descending as it did when it took a sharp turn. "It's so different from an airplane," I said, grabbing Paxon's hands like I had when we left Butler Ranch.

When he brought one to his lips and kissed my palm, I felt a surge of heat spread right through me and settle between my legs.

I knew Paxon was right when he'd said we should wait before he left on his mission. It hadn't been easy, though. Every inch of my body longed to feel his touch.

I'd read enough books to have an idea of what it would be like when we were finally together. What I hoped it would be like, anyway. It wasn't like I had any girlfriends I could ask how accurate those books were.

I guess I could've asked Stella, but she was marrying my brother. That would be way too embarrassing. Or Nina and Lucy, but I hardly knew them.

There was only one person I could think of that I trusted enough to talk to about sex, and he was sitting right beside me. I knew, without any doubt at all, that he'd tell me in a way that didn't make me feel stupid or inexperienced, just like he'd talked to me about every-thing else.

He slipped off my headset, took his off too, and handed them both to Naughton while we waited for the blades of the helicopter to stop spinning.

"I would love to know what you were thinking about a minute ago," Paxon whispered in my ear.

"I can show you."

"Yeah?"

I took his hand and kissed it, pressing the lines on his palm with my tongue like he had to mine. Paxon's eye-lids half closed, and he leaned forward and kissed me.

"Hey, you two," said Naughton. "It's gonna be dark in about three minutes, and you're going to have to wait until tomorrow to see your view."

"Sorry," I mumbled, following Paxon when he climbed out. "Where are we?" I asked, spinning in a circle.

"This area used to be where Hearst warehoused all the stuff he brought in from around the world to put up in his castle on the hill. A couple of years ago, my mom bought this place and had it turned into a little seaside getaway for her and my dad. His mother and father met when they both worked for Hearst."

"That's so romantic," I said, looking first out at the ocean and then at the little house that looked like it had been right here forever, lovingly cared for by people like Laird and Sorcha.

"Come on in, and I'll show you around."

"Do they just leave it unlocked?" I asked when he pulled the sliding door to the side.

"Nah, Kade was here a little while ago, dropping off your stuff." He pointed to bags I recognized as Paxon's.

"Wow," I said when he turned the lights on. "It looks so cozy." It was decorated similarly to the house we'd visited at Butler Ranch, with mission-style furniture.

"My wife, Bradley—you didn't meet her, because she's at a wine festival this week. Anyway, she helped my ma decorate."

"It's lovely."

Naughton picked up a set of keys that were sitting on one of the end tables in the living room that looked out over the ocean. "This one is for the front door. You lock the slider from the inside, and this one is for the car you'll find in the garage. Be right back." He ran out of the house and over to the helicopter.

"Can you believe this?" I asked Paxon.

He grabbed my hand and pulled me into a hug. "I can't think about anything besides your tongue on my hand, Flynn. Nothing. My mind is blank. We could be on top of a volcano, and I wouldn't know it."

"Almost forgot this," said Naughton, bringing in a basket. "It's your breakfast, and there's more in the refrigerator. I stocked the place with beer and wine too."

I nudged Paxon when it looked like Naughton was getting ready to leave.

"Thank you so much. So, we can stay here tonight?" I asked.

"You can stay here as long as you want." Naughton walked to another room and turned on more lights. He motioned to what looked like a dining room table. "I told my mother that you'd probably just look stuff up on the internet, but she insisted I go pick up brochures and maps from the bookstore in Cambria." He picked up an envelope and handed it to Paxon.

"Thanks."

Naughton put his hand on Paxon's shoulder. "You okay, man?"

"Yeah, uh, just kind of overwhelmed at the moment."

"That's from my brother. I'm sure it'll explain some of it, at least."

"Thank you so much," I repeated when it didn't appear Paxon had found his words yet.

"I'll head out now. Have fun!"

"Paxon," I whispered, bumping him with my hip.

"Right. Uh, you have fun too."

Naughton shook his head and laughed as he walked out to the helicopter.

"I can't even believe how beautiful—"

Before I realized what was happening, Paxon had me in his arms. "What are you doing?" I giggled. "Put me down before you hurt yourself."

"I need to be next to you. All of me next to all of you. Think the bedroom is in this direction?"

"I guess we'll find out."

He carried me down a hallway that turned to the right, and pushed open the first door we came to with his knee. Like in the living room, there was a wall of windows that looked out over the ocean. Paxon walked over and stood in front of them.

"You can put me down now."

"No."

I giggled again. "Why not?"

"I like having you in my arms."

"I'm too heavy."

"You're perfect."

46

Irish

In the same way I knew we shouldn't make love the night before I left for China, I knew tonight we would. It just felt right. Everything felt right. I couldn't remember any other time in my life when there wasn't anywhere else I wanted to be, nothing else I wanted to be doing, no one else I wanted to be with.

All I needed in the world, I held in my arms. I kissed her again and again, like I planned to do all night, tomorrow, and tomorrow night. Hell, I planned to spend the rest of my life kissing Flynn. Every chance I got.

"Paxon?"

"Mm-hmm?"

"We need to talk."

I carried her over to the bed and gently rested her body on it. I stretched out behind her and slowly lowered the zipper on the back of her dress.

"What are you doing?" she asked.

"Listening." I moved her hair out of my way, leaned forward, and ran my tongue from the base of her neck down her spine until I came to the clasp on her bra. I released it and kept my trail of kisses going until I reached the small of her back. "You aren't talking, Flynn."

"Talk? I can't even think with you doing that."

"Now you know how I felt at the end of our helicopter ride. I doubt I could've told you my name if you'd asked."

"Oh, God," she groaned when I lowered her panties and kissed the dimples right above her ass.

"Do you want me to stop, Flynn?"

"If you stop, I'll die. I just know it."

I got on my knees and turned her over. I helped her take off her dress, remove her bra, and let my gaze linger on her panties.

As I did with her back, I trailed kisses from her lips all the way down the front of her body. When I reached the lace of her panties, I moved them aside.

"Paxon," she groaned when I slid my fingers inside and parted her folds. I touched her clit with the tip of my tongue, and she bucked beneath me.

"What...what...are you doing?"

"Enjoying the hell out of every inch of your body."

"But—"

"Shh, my precious Flynn. The only thing you need to do is relax and let yourself enjoy it."

"Paxon, I never..."

She shuddered when I blew on her wetness.

"I need…"

I eased a finger inside her. "What do you need? Tell me, Flynn."

Her head rolled from side to side. "I have no idea. Just more."

I added a second finger, gently pumping in and out while she writhed beneath me.

"Paxon, please. I need to see you. I need to feel you."

"You still aren't talking."

"This. This was it."

"It?"

She reached down and stopped my hand's movement. "You and me. Tonight. Now. I want to know. I need to know. I don't care what happens tomorrow; just don't make me wait any longer."

As I kissed my way up her body, she squirmed when I reached her soft tummy, so I lingered there, loving on every bit of her flesh.

When I reached her lips, she parted them and I thrust my tongue in her mouth. Her hands landed on my still-clothed ass.

"You need to take off your clothes and—"

"There are a couple of things we need to talk about before that happens."

"Okay," she said, her eyes darting between mine.

"First, I do care what happens tomorrow and every day after that."

"I didn't mean—"

I put my fingertips on her lips, the same fingers that had been inside her, and she groaned.

"You and I were made for each other. I can't say with certainty that I believed in God until I met you. Then I knew a higher power had to exist because you, my precious Flynn, are an angel. I'm never letting you go. Never. As long as there is breath left in my body, I want you next to me. This will probably sound crazy to you, but there hasn't been a time when we've been together and I haven't known that in my heart. Even from the first moment we met."

"I felt the same."

"I don't know what the future will bring other than you and I will be together."

"I want that more than anything."

"Enough to marry me?"

"Yes."

Her certainty, her lack of hesitation, her absolute acceptance made my heart beat faster. "I love you. You know that?"

"I do and I love you."

"Your brothers are going to think we're crazy. Either that or they'll want to hurt me."

"If there's anything I've learned since my dad got sick it's that all my brothers want is for me to be happy." She wiggled her hips. "So, what about you getting naked?"

"I'm sorry, but we have to wait, Flynn."

Her eyes opened wide. "Until we're married?" she gasped.

I smiled and shook my head. "Until tomorrow and I can buy condoms."

She bit her bottom lip. "That was one of the things I wanted to tell you."

I raised a brow.

"I brought some."

"You did?"

She nodded.

I rolled off the bed, stood, and pulled my shirt over my head. Flynn rolled too and sat on the edge of the bed in front of me.

"Let me do it," she said, unfastening my belt. She slowly and gently lowered the zipper, and I could feel the heat of her breath on my skin when she pushed my boxer briefs down. I fisted my hand in her hair when she leaned forward and kissed the tip of my cock.

"Where are the condoms?" I groaned when she swirled her tongue around my hardness. There would be plenty of time for us to pleasure each other's bodies with our mouths and hands. Right now, I had to be inside of her. As much for her as for me. There would be pain, and I wanted to put that behind us and only experience the pleasure.

I pulled away, and she pouted. "But I wanted—"

"There's something I want more. Tell me where the condoms are. I need to be inside you, Flynn. Deep inside you."

Her eyes hooded, and she pointed to the doorway. "In the outside pocket of the blue bag."

I grabbed a handful and tore one open as I made my way into the bedroom. I realized then that the house had no window coverings. Something I didn't care about but wondered if Flynn would. Selfishly, I didn't want to tell her, especially when I came back into the bedroom and found her waiting spread wide open with her hand between her legs.

I dropped the remaining condom packets on the floor, rolled one on, and knelt in front of her.

"We have no curtains to close," I said, looking over my shoulder.

"Paxon, I wouldn't care if we were out in the open with a hundred people watching us. If you don't put that inside me right now, I'll have to take matters into my own hands."

"It looked like you already were."

"Quit teasing me," she half groaned, half shouted.

"We're going to take this slow. If it hurts too much, just tell me." I positioned myself at her entrance. My body shook with desire as I eased in. Flynn put her hands on my ass like she had earlier, except this time, I was naked. Before I realized what she had planned, she thrust onto me, holding my ass in place with all her might. "So impatient," I said, starting to move my hips. "Did that hurt?"

"It's a distant memory at this point. Just keep doing what you're doing."

"Like that?" I asked, alternating between rotating my hips and moving in and out of her drenched heat.

Her eyes met mine, and she held her breath. "It's happening." I picked up my pace when she arched her neck and closed her eyes.

"Look at me. Let me see you," I said, knowing I couldn't hold back any longer. "I love you, Flynn."

"I love you, Paxon."

47

Flynn

After spending five days and nights in Sorcha and Laird's house by the sea, I asked Paxon to contact them to make sure it was okay that we were still there.

"She wants to talk to you," he said, handing me the phone.

"Hello?"

"You stay as long as you want, lass. I can hear in your voices how content you both are."

"Be careful. We might want to stay forever."

"I wouldn't mind at all, my dear. You both deserve every happiness."

"You are too kind, Sorcha."

"Do you have enough food, Flynn? I could send Laird with another basket if you'd like."

"Thank you so much, but we're fine. We've even gone into town a couple of times." Paxon's phone beeped. "Oh, there's another call coming in."

"You best answer. Stay as long at the house as you'd like, and let me know if you need anything."

I hit the button to end that call and accept the other and handed the phone to Paxon.

He looked at the screen and sat down next to me on the bed. "Hey, Doc."

I pointed to my chest and out to the other room, but Paxon shook his head.

"I wanted to give you an update on Harris." I was close enough that I could hear every word.

"Go ahead."

"After talking it over with Money, we're moving him down to Santa Barbara County, where he'll be in a criminal psychiatric facility located not far from my house in Montecito. At this point, it's impossible to determine whether he's truly insane, if it's temporary after what he experienced in the black jail, or if he's brilliant enough to be playing us. Believing it's one of the first two, we want to get him the help he needs. It's self-serving, of course, but still the right thing to do."

"What about Fisk?"

"Singing like a little canary."

"I hope Money is getting what we need."

"It's over, Irish. If I didn't believe it, I'd never say it."

"I hope you're right."

"Don't hope. Believe."

With those words, Paxon's eyes met mine.

"I gotta go, Doc. Thanks for the update."

"Before you hang up, did you read my letter?"

"Crap. Sorry, forgot all about it."

I could hear him laughing. "Glad to hear it. Enjoy yourself. Tell Flynn to enjoy herself too."

"Thanks, Doc," I said.

"Oh, you're there. Hey, do me a favor and put in a good word for K19, would ya? We'd love to have Paxon on our team."

"That's up to him, but if it means we get to come back and visit this sweet little house by the sea, it might work in your favor."

"Bye, Doc," said Paxon, ending the call.

"How are you feeling?" I asked.

"Free. Completely, thoroughly free."

* * *

Paxon and I spent a month at Laird and Sorcha's seaside cottage. We took day trips up and down the coast but ended every night in each other's arms in the bed where we'd first made love.

"You haven't said anything about returning to Colorado, and I haven't wanted to ask, but do you need to?"

I shrugged. "I suppose I should, even though I wish we didn't have to leave."

"We don't. Not until you say you're ready."

"Maybe a few more days." While he showered, I called Cord, like I had once each week.

"We're doing fine," he said instead of hello, and I laughed.

"You don't even miss me?"

"Do you miss us?"

"Not so much."

He laughed. "You're making up for all those years you never left. You probably accumulated six months' vacation time, at least."

"There's something I want to talk to you about."

"Shoot."

"Paxon and I are getting married."

"Well, yeehaw!" he shouted. "Flynn's getting married," I heard him say. In the background, I could hear my brothers hooting and hollering.

"Would you be upset if we just had a simple ceremony here?"

"I don't know where here is, but I'll speak on behalf of all four of us. All we care about is your happiness, Flynn."

"That's what I told Paxon."

"Whenever you decide to come home, we'll throw a big party."

"A small party."

"Whatever."

"I want to ask you something else."

"Good God, girl. Get to it."

"We want to move into the cabin Paxon stayed in."

"Are you sure you don't want the main house?"

"What about you, Holt, and Porter?"

"We could move out."

I thought it over for a minute. "The cabin is where we want to start our life together."

"I think you already did that, but you have your pick of anywhere on the ranch, sis." I heard my oldest brother say something in the background, but I couldn't make it out.

"Sorry, Buck says you can't have the old farmhouse, but everything else is fair game."

I laughed. "You tell Buck I'm good with that." Paxon came out of the bathroom with a towel wrapped around his waist. When I wiggled my eyebrows, he dropped it.

"I gotta go, but I love you all, and we'll see you... sometime." I ended the call and tossed the phone on the floor when the man who would soon be my husband stalked my way.

Epilogue

Irish
Two Months Later

One week after she told her brothers and I told Cope and Ali, Flynn and I were married at Butler Ranch in what we'd planned to be a small ceremony by "our" bench in the vineyards.

No one confirmed it, but I guessed it was Sorcha who had arranged for so many of our friends and family to join us, including most of the men and women who had been a part of bringing down Argead once and for all.

Buck and Stella could only stay one day because of the bizarre terms of my wife's father's will, but it didn't take away our joy of having them, her other three brothers, along with Cope and Ali with us. The biggest surprise was when I saw Lynx, Emme, and Saint walk up with Money McTiernan.

Decker apologized for missing it but had a damned good reason. He and Mila's baby boy, who they named Huck, had finally arrived. Doc joked that his absence would give him time to convince me to join K19, but

Decker knew better. I'd been honest with him about not being ready to make any decisions.

We'd spent our honeymoon in the cabin where we began our life together even before we knew that's what we were doing. I'd never been happier in my life. In fact, I hadn't known a life like the one I was leading was even possible.

Instead of spending my days thinking about missions or agents dying or even world politics, I learned to ride a horse, mend fences, tend cattle, refurbish cabins, and be part of a family.

I ate every meal in the dining hall with my wife when she was working, at our own table for two no one else dared sit at.

In a few months, we'd add a couple of high chairs when our little family grew from two to four, since Flynn was pregnant with twins.

"Are you sure about traveling to Washington?" I asked when she and I crawled into bed and she snuggled in my arms.

"If you think I'm going to stay here while my beloved husband is awarded the Presidential Medal of Freedom, you're crazy."

"It isn't that big of a deal."

Flynn rolled her eyes. "Oh yeah? So why is it that everyone who was at our wedding, along with a few who weren't, is flying in for it?"

"I still think Cope should be receiving it too."

"Maybe one day he will, but tomorrow is your day. Let us all love on you, Paxon."

Little by little, my wife taught me to accept honor, praise, and love, and I did the same for her. My chest swelled with pride as I watched her blossom into a confident, self-assured force of nature.

Whenever I thought about how we met, I couldn't help but shake my head at the irony of it. The worst thing I'd ever gone through in my life, resulted in the best thing ever happening to me.

"Where did you go?" she asked, stroking my cheek with her finger.

"Just thinking what a lucky man I am."

"You know what I need?"

I chuckled, already knowing what she was going to say. It had become a code for when our bodies couldn't stand another moment not being joined together.

"Let me guess," I teased. "You want to be Irished."

"You got it." Flynn smiled and slid her hand down the front of my body.

Keep reading for a sneak peek
at the next book
in the Invincibles series—
SAINTED!

1

Saint

I was one of the people chosen to interrogate the man the Chinese called a "whistleblower," and everyone in the intelligence world referred to as a bloody traitor—the nicest words said about him, in fact.

It was one of a handful of times being British served me with the team that was responsible for extracting Daniel "Xander" Harris from the black jail in Gongqing Forest Park where he was being held, and was primarily made up of men who were once with the CIA.

Given Xander's betrayal of his country was fueled by his hatred for it, sending in a Brit over a Yank proved useful. That the Chinese had brought him to the brink of death when his "asylum" turned into detainment, made the man even more willing to give up the secrets we'd wanted him to.

I was the sole MI6 agent who had gone along on the extraction mission. It had taken begging the lead agent, Paxon "Irish" Warrick, to allow me to.

Begging was not something normally in my wheelhouse. At least not before. My life had changed, though.

I was no longer the *bon vivant* I once was. At thirty, I was young for a has-been, which meant a rebranding was in order.

If one was to ask anyone in the espionage community about me, the first word likely to be used was *lothario*. *Ineffective* would certainly be in the top three. *Former* MI6 agent would fill the remaining slot.

As I sat in on the meetings during which the mission was planned, I felt the disdain of my peers. I hadn't been imagining it; their lack of respect was as heavy as it was thick.

I'd used the derision to convince Irish to let me go along. It was a feeling he'd experienced much longer than I had. For several months he, like Xander, was believed to be a double agent—a traitor—someone to be reviled not just by those he worked with but the entirety of the democratic world.

What I'd said was I needed to be on the mission. Yes, *needed*, I'd confirmed when he questioned my word choice.

If I were able to prove my worth, perhaps one of the two private intelligence and security firms who had jointly been assigned the mission, would offer me a job. I'd even consider a contractor position with the CIA, if it came down to it. Although that would be a harder sell.

It wasn't just my professional reputation I needed to fix, though. What people thought of me personally was just as dire. What was I especially good at? Seducing women—ala James Bond—I'd heard frequently.

Perhaps when I set out as a member of Her Majesty's Secret Intelligence Service, I'd fancied myself to be the real-life version of 007. I'd relied on my looks and charm throughout my life. Not doing so was a hard habit to break.

That I'd been invited to the after-party to celebrate Irish's receipt of the Presidential Medal of Freedom, I saw as a win.

While I'd promised myself I would take it easy, the alcohol flowed freely as we celebrated the end of a yearslong mission as much as we did Warrick receiving his country's high honor.

The gathering had been arranged to take place in the hotel where most of us were staying. Thus, several of the group assembled were drunker than I was. Not that being "less drunk" was something I could tout as an accomplishment.

I approached the bar to order what I'd promised myself would be my last drink and noticed a woman—a stunning woman—sitting alone, her glass nearly empty.

"May I get you another?" I asked.

"Um, I promised myself this would be my last," she said, lifting the drink that was now only ice.

"I've made myself the same promise," I said, motioning to the bartender. "One more and then I'm cut off for the night."

"I guess I could have one more."

Three drinks later, for both of us, we frantically tore at one another's clothes in the elevator that would take us to the top floor and to my hotel room.

Like my resolve not to overindulge alcohol, I vowed instead that *tomorrow,* I would also curb my carnal excessiveness.

"Tell me your name," I said as I had for the last two hours without success.

"No names," she responded, tugging at my belt buckle once we were in my room.

When I woke the next morning after very little sleep but hours of mind-blowing sex, I wasn't surprised to see my lover had sneaked out sometime between dawn, when we both passed out from exhaustion, and now, a little after ten.

I stretched my arms over my head and rolled out of bed. "One day at a time," I muttered to myself as I looked in the bathroom mirror at the man who looked far more like my father than the way I saw myself.

Two hours later, I walked onto the lift that would take me to the office of the newly named CIA director. Once there, I would request permission, and ask for help, in locating a Chinese national. The man was the son of a British diplomat and MI6 asset who I'd been responsible for protecting the last two years.

Taking on the personal mission was yet another item on the list of my path to redemption. If I were to find the man who had been missing for nine years and whom the US had a great interest in questioning then maybe I'd be able to check "professional reputation improved" off my list.

I stepped out when the doors opened and, to my utter dismay, came face-to-face with the woman I'd spent the previous night with.

"Good afternoon," I said, approaching the gorgeous creature who had gone ghostly pale the moment our eyes met. "I'm Niven St. Thomas. Most call me Saint. What is your name?"

About the Author

USA Today and Amazon Top 15 Bestselling Author Heather Slade writes shamelessly sexy, edge-of-your seat romantic suspense.

She gave herself the gift of writing a book for her own birthday one year. Forty-plus books later (and counting), she's having the time of her life.

The women Slade writes are self-confident, strong, with wills of their own, and hearts as big as the Colorado sky. The men are sublimely sexy, seductive alphas who rise to the challenge of capturing the sweet soul of a woman whose heart they'll hold in the palm of their hand forever. Add in a couple of neck-snapping twists and turns, a page-turning mystery, and a swoon-worthy HEA, and you'll be holding one of her books in your hands.

She loves to hear from my readers. You can contact her at heather@heatherslade.com

To keep up with her latest news and releases, please visit her website at www.heatherslade.com to sign up for her newsletter.

MORE FROM AUTHOR HEATHER SLADE

BUTLER RANCH

Kade's Worth

Brodie

Maddox

Naughton

Mercer

Kade

Christmas at Butler Ranch

WICKED WINEMAKERS' BALL

Coming soon:

Brix

Ridge

Press

K19 SECURITY SOLUTIONS

Razor

Gunner

Mistletoe

Mantis

Dutch

Striker

Monk

Halo

Tackle

Onyx

K19 SHADOW OPERATIONS

Code Name: Ranger

Code Name: Diesel

Coming soon:

Code Name: Wasp

Code Name: Cowboy

THE ROYAL AGENTS OF MI6

The Duke and the Assassin

The Lord and the Spy

The Commoner and the Correspondent

The Rancher and the Lady

THE INVINCIBLES

Decked

Undercover Agent

Edged

Grinded

Riled

Handled

Smoked

Bucked

Irished

Sainted

Hammered

Coming soon:

Ripped

THE UNSTOPPABLES

Coming soon:

Furied

Vexed

COWBOYS OF CRESTED BUTTE

A Cowboy Falls

A Cowboy's Dance

A Cowboy's Kiss

A Cowboy Stays

A Cowboy Wins

Made in the USA
Middletown, DE
19 May 2022

65966105R00215